Hell Come Sundown

Hell Come Sundown

A Dark Ranger Story

Nancy A. Collins

OPEN ROAD
INTEGRATED MEDIA
NEW YORK

ISBN: 978-1-5040-7480-3

This edition published in 2022 by Open Road Integrated Media, Inc.
180 Maiden Lane
New York, NY 10038
www.openroadmedia.com

To a good friend and excellent Texan: Joe R. Lansdale

Hell Come Sundown

Chapter One

TEXAS, 1869:

Hiram McKinney glanced up from his Bible as the cherry-wood mantle clock chimed eight o'clock. The timepiece, with its hinged convex glass lens and elegantly embossed Arabic numerals, was one of the few luxuries that had survived the trip from Tennessee to Texas.

"It's time you got off to bed, young man," Hiram told his son, who was toiling over his *McGuffey's Reader* workbook.

"Please, Pa, can't I stay up a lit'l while longer?"

"You heard yore daddy, Jacob," Miriam McKinney countered, without looking up from the sock she was darning.

"Yes ma'am," Jake replied glumly, setting aside his schoolwork as he scooted his chair away from the table. The seven-year-old walked over to where his parents sat before the fieldstone fireplace to bid them good night. His mother put aside her sewing and leaned forward, pecking her son the cheek.

"Night, Jake."

"Night, Maw. Night, Pa," the boy said, turning to his father.

Mr. McKinney glanced up from his reading. He gave his son a fond smile and a nod. While Jake would never be too old for his Maw to

3

kiss, Hiram had recently decided that the boy was beyond such molly-coddling.

As Jake headed for his room, Mrs. McKinney called out after him one last time: "Pleasant dreams, sweetheart."

Neither parent saw the boy flinch.

The McKinneys came to Texas fifteen years before, setting down stakes on prime ranching land along the Nueces River, near Laredo. For the first five years they lived out of a one-room cabin. Then, as time moved on and they gradually became more prosperous, Hiram added a second room, so that he and Miriam no longer had to sleep where they ate. Three years later, Jake was born.

Jacob was not the McKinney's first child, but he was the only one to survive the cradle, his older brother and sister having succumbed to disease before they got their first tooth. For the first three years of his life he slept in the family bed. Then he was moved to a pallet in the corner. When Jake reached the age of five, it was decided that he was old enough to move to the lofted area above the communal room. For the next two years, Jake drifted off to sleep listening to his parents discuss their day's activities or plan what needed to be done to keep the homestead running smooth.

As the McKinney family's fortunes continued to rise, Hiram decided they could afford constructing a room for their son, placing it opposite their own, so that the layout of the house resembled a capital T.

Most boys Jake's age would have been thrilled to have their very own room. And, at first, Jake was very excited by the prospect. But all that changed after his first week of sleeping alone. The very first night, his screams woke up the house. His father charged into the room in his long johns, shotgun in hand, convinced that Comanches were dragging his son out the window. Once Hiram realized that was not the case, he cussed to beat the band.

When Jake told his parents about the thing that came out from under his bed, they listened for a moment then exchanged looks. Pa was more than a little put out by the whole thing, but when he saw how frightened Jake was, he made a show of getting down on his hands and knees to prove there wasn't a boogey man hiding under the bed.

Maw McKinney said it was only natural for a young boy to be frightened the first time he had to sleep on his own. All his life, Jake had slept within earshot of his family. Sleeping by himself in a separate part of the house would take some getting used to. His father had grudgingly agreed to that point—after all, he himself hadn't slept in a separate room until after he was married, and even then he'd never truly slept alone.

However, as Jake's night terrors continued, his father's tolerance rapidly eroded. Pa was of the opinion that Maw was mollycoddling the boy, where Maw felt that Pa was in too big a hurry to make a man out of a child.

This was not a new argument between the McKinneys, but it grew with each passing birthday. Since Jake loved his parents with all his heart, knowing he was the reason for them not getting along tore him up something fierce. Jake wanted to be a man and make his daddy proud, really he did. But there was something going on that neither of his parents truly understood.

The reason for his night terrors wasn't bad dreams or fear of being alone. The simple fact of the matter was that his bedroom was haunted. Jake wasn't real certain how that could be, as no one ever lived in it before. He had always been of the impression that it took someone dying in a place to make it haunted, but apparently that wasn't a hard-and-fast rule.

However, he had learned that whatever it was that lived under his bed did follow a pattern of behavior. Whatever it was didn't come out every night—just those that coincided with the dark of the moon. He also knew that the thing was scared away by screaming and light, even if it was the weakest candle flame. Just a hint of lamplight appearing under the crack of the door as his mother came to check on him was enough to cause the apparition to fold in upon itself like a lady's lace fan.

At first he thought that the thing that haunted the room could only harm him if he looked at it, so he slept curled up in a tight little ball, the covers pulled up over his head. At first this seemed to stymie the thing from under the bed, but it eventually figured out that it could force him to throw back the blankets by sitting atop his huddled form until its weight threatened to suffocate him. As terrible as the creature was to look upon, the knowledge that the thing was sprawled across his bed was even more horrifying.

After the first couple of weeks, his father forbade his mother from checking on him whenever he cried out during the night. When it became clear his mother would no longer be coming to his aid, Jake realized that it was up to him, and him alone, to solve his problem.

He at first attempted to battle the monster by keeping the lamp burning beside his bed all night long. This worked at first—until his father began complaining about the amount of oil that was being wasted. The general store was in Cochina Lake, over ten miles away, and the McKinneys only went there once every six weeks. Because of the increase in consumption, they were close to being out of fuel, and with two weeks to go before the next trip.

Jake's nights were seldom restful, and his dreams rarely pleasant. Even on those nights he was not haunted by the thing from under the bed, he slept fitfully, waking every time a timber groaned or a branch scraped the side of the house. Still, as bad as things were, he could not bring himself to tell his parents the truth of his situation. For one, he knew they would not believe him, and another, he did not wish his father to see him as a frightened little boy. If being born and raised in Texas had taught him anything, it was self-reliance. This was his problem, by damn, and it was up to him to solve it, come what may.

The light cast by Jake's lamp chased the shadows back into their respective corners as he entered the darkened room. The curtains his mother had fashioned from old flour sacks were pulled tightly shut against the moonless night. Aside from the bed, the only other furnishings in the room were a nightstand, a footstool and a double chifferobe, since the room had no closets. The walls were made from planks his Pa had cut at the local sawmill, and the chinks between the boards were caulked with river clay to keep the wind out. That the solitary window in the room boasted panes of glass instead of waxed cloth was a testament to the McKinney family's newfound prosperity in this unlikely promised land.

Jake carefully placed the lamp on the nightstand and began to undress, neatly folding his clothes over the foot of the bed as he did so.

He removed his nightshirt from its place under his pillow and pulled it on over his head. Jake gave the room one last apprehensive look before blowing out the light and jumping under the covers. The interlaced ropes that supported the mattress groaned slightly as he tried to get comfortable under the pile of quilts that covered the bed.

Instead of burrowing down to the heart of the bed like a prairie dog—like he usually did—Jake lay on his back and stared at the ceiling, as rigid as the rafters above his head. His arms were stiffly extended along his sides atop the covers, his hands balled into tight fists as if prepared for a fight . . .

A finger as long and thin as a pitchfork tine emerged from the shadowy region under the bed. It was followed by its brothers, each as long and narrow as the first. The spidery, overlong digits were joined to a wide, flat palm, which was attached to a bony wrist. The fingers hooked themselves into claws, digging into the floorboards as the thing dragged itself clear of the bed. It stood up once it was free, unfolding itself like a pocketknife. Its knobby back made a clicking sound as it shrugged its shoulders, locking its spine into place. Although the thing before him filled him with terror, Jake bit his tongue to keep from crying out. The time had come for him to face that which frightened him and become its master.

It was pale as a frog's belly, with skin like that found on a pitcher of milk that's been left to sit too long. Its body was hairless, save for the tangle of lank, greasy curls that hung from its lopsided head like a nest of dead snakes. Its legs were as long and thin as tent poles, and bent backward at the knee so that it seemed to be both walking away from and toward its prey at the same time.

The face, if you could call it one, was toad-like in appearance, with wide, rubbery lips, a pair of slits in place of a nose, and two huge, blood red eyes that glowed like an angry cat's. When the thing smacked its lips, Jake could see the inside of its mouth was ringed with jagged teeth.

As the fiend stared down at Jake, the boy saw a brief glimmer of surprise in its hideous eyes. Clearly it had not expected its victim to be so exposed. Still, it knew better than to question its good fortune. The thing moved so that it loomed over the boy, bending low so that its hideous face was mere inches from Jake's own, its spiderlike talons poised to spear the terrified child's eyeballs.

The horror that hovered before him blinked an inner eyelid, and the nasal slits that served as its nose dilated sharply, catching scent of the subtle change in the chemistry of fear. Emitting a low growl, the thing abruptly turned its head on its shoulders like an owl, so that it was staring over its shoulders at the chifferobe.

The moment the monster took its murderous gaze off him, Jake kicked back the bedclothes, causing the creature to swivel its head back in his direction. "*Now!*" the boy screamed at the top of his lungs. "*Do it now!*"

The doors to the wardrobe flew open with a bang, and out of its depths stepped a man dressed all in black, from his scuffed cowboy boots and floor-length duster to the hat on his head. He brandished a pistol in hands so pale it looked as if they had been dipped in whitewash. His face was equally pallid, save for his eyes, which burned like red-hot coals dropped in a snow bank. About the pale man's neck was cinched a bolo made from a polished stone the color of blood.

"Step back from the boy, critter," the pale man said in a voice that sounded as if it were coming from the bottom of a well.

The thing from under the bed flipped its head back around on its shoulders and snarled at the intruder, displaying a ring of razor-sharp teeth. A sane man would have fainted dead away or fled the scene, but the pale man opened fire instead. The thing clutched its midsection, a look of confusion and pain on its hideous face, before collapsing onto the floor.

"You did it!" Jake shouted gleefully, jumping up and down on the bed. "You killed him!"

"Don't get too excited there, son—you can't really kill these critters," the pale man replied, holstering his pistols.

There was a loud slam as the door to Jake's room flew open and Hiram McKinney entered the room, galluses dangling from his pants, shotgun ready. "Who in hell are you, mister, and what are you doing in my boy's room?" he thundered.

The pale man raised his hands slow and easy, so as not to tense the rancher's trigger finger. "The name's Hell. Sam Hell. And I'm here at your son's request."

"That's right, Pa!" Jake said excitedly, jumping up and down on the bed. "This here's the Dark Ranger! He come to get rid of the monster! See?!? It's real! It's really real! And it came out from under my bed, just like I tole ya!"

Hiram looked to where his son was pointing. "Sweet baby Jesus!" he gasped, his eyes started from their sockets. "What in Heaven's name is that?"

"Heaven has nothing to do with it, Mr. McKinney," Sam Hell replied. "May I put my hands down now?"

"Hiram, honey? What is going on in here—?" Mrs. McKinney poked her head around the doorjamb, a homespun shawl about her shoulders and her hair gathered into her nightcap. She gave out with a squeal of horror upon seeing the thing sprawled across the floor.

"Tell you the truth, Miriam—I have no earthly idea what's going on," her husband admitted.

"I sent for him, Pa! I saw his advertisement in the back of this magazine, and I wrote him, telling him what was wrong, and he wrote back and said he could help and tole me what to do what to when he got here!"

"Excuse me, folks—but as I've been trying to explain to your boy here, this dance ain't done yet."

The man called Hell stepped over the body of the fiend on the floor, pushed back the sackcloth curtains and opened the window, which swung inward on a hinge. A second later a woman, dressed in the fringed riding chaps and beaded pectoral of an Indian warrior, clambered over the sill.

"*Comanche!*" McKinney shouted, lifting his weapon.

Hell turned and grabbed the barrel of the shotgun in one milk white hand, forcing its muzzle to the floor. Hiram tried to yank the weapon free from the pale stranger's grasp, but there was no budging it.

"Yes, Pretty Woman is a Comanche." Hell said matter-of-factly. "And I would kindly appreciate it if you did not point your gun at a lady—especially one who happens to be my business partner."

The Comanche woman acted as if she did not see or hear what was going on about her as she knelt beside the creature on the floor. Muttering a chant under her breath, she removed a grass-rope lariat tied about her waist and hogtied the unconscious creature like a steer ready for branding. Just as she finished trussing it up, the thing made a wailing sound, like that of a wounded elk, and began to struggle. Mrs. McKinney screamed and snatched her son off the bed, clutching him to her in an attempt to shield him. Hiram McKinney tried to pull his shotgun free of the stranger's grip in order to fire on the thing, but it was still held fast.

"There's no need to panic, folks," Hell said calmly. "Pretty's got it under control."

The medicine woman learned in close to the fiend's wildly gnashing mouth. She raised a clenched fist to her lips and blew a quick burst of air into it. A cloud of grayish white powder enveloped the creature's face. It abruptly ceased its howling and became as limp as wet laundry.

"Is it dead?" Mrs. McKinney asked, her curiosity having overcome her dread.

"Like I told your boy—there's no killing such critters," Hell said flatly, letting go of Hiram's shotgun. "You might as well try and murder a stone or stab the sea. Best you can do is make sure it can't do you harm."

Pretty Woman removed a leather bag from her belt and emptied its contents, mostly dried herbs and other less identifiable artifacts, onto the floor. She glanced up her partner with eyes as dark and bright as a raven's, and he nodded in return.

"Come along, folks," Hell said, motioning for the others to leave the room. "We better leave Pretty to finish her ghost-breaking in peace. Something tells me y'all could do with a cup of coffee right about now."

Chapter Two

HIRAM MCKINNEY SAT in his favorite chair, his shotgun resting across his knees, while Mrs. McKinney busied herself with making coffee. He stared at the pale-skinned stranger who called himself Hell, who was sitting opposite him in his wife's rocking chair. At first Hiram had thought the stranger was an albino, but now that he was able to get a closer look, he could see that Hell's complexion was more like that of the consumptives who had come out west for the Cure. Uncertain of how to proceed in such an unusual situation, he finally decided there was no wrong way to go about it, so he opted to grab the bull by the horns.

"Jake said something about him writing you—?"

"Yes, sir. That he did."

"Here, Pa—this is what I was talking about." Jake handed his father a copy of *Pickman's Illustrated Serials*, which was tightly rolled in order to fit in the boy's back pocket.

Hiram took the periodical and flattened it out as best he could across his knee. He frowned at the lurid illustration that adorned the front cover, which showed a band of outlaws shooting up a town, each of whom had swooning damsels and bags of loot clutched in whichever hand that did not hold a smoking six-shooter. Floating over the desperadoes' heads was the title of the lead story, in ornately engraved script: *The Tortuga Hill Gang Rides Again.*

"You been wasting good money on penny dreadfuls?" Hiram said sternly, glowering at his son in disapproval.

"Far be it from me to step in between a father and his son," Hell said. "But don't you reckon you're being a tad harsh on the boy, considering the situation?"

Hiram opened his mouth, as if to argue to point, then realized the foolishness of it. "I reckon you're right on that point, mister."

"Here, Pa—here's where I saw his advertisement." Jake pointed to a quarter-page ad, located just below the one for Dr. Mirablis's Amazing Electric Truss. Unlike the other advertisements, it did not boast steel-engraved pictures or florid script, even though what it claimed to be selling was far more arcane than the patent medicines and seed catalogs that surrounded it.

Troubled by Specters, Ghosts and Phantoms? Fear No More! There Is Help! Call For The Dark Ranger: Ghost Breaking A Specialty! No Spook Too Small, No Fiend Too Fierce! Write Care of: Box 1, Golgotha, Texas. Our Motto: 'One Wraith, One Ranger.'

"Dark Ranger?" Hiram rubbed his forehead, baffled by what he was reading. He glanced over at the man seated across from him with something akin to awe. "You a Texas Ranger, mister?"

A look of profound sorrow flickered across Hell's face and was quickly gone, like a cloud scudding across the moon. "I was. Back before the troubles."

Hiram raised an eyebrow. "Cortina?"

Hell took a deep breath and nodded, as if the very memory caused him pain. "Yep. I was at Rio Grande City. Now that the Rangers have been replaced with those carpetbaggin' State Police, I break ghosts and scare off things that go bump in the night."

"Any man who rode with Captain Ford is more than welcome in my home," Hiram said, putting aside his shotgun. He stood and offered Hell his hand. "And I am eternally grateful for you helpin' out my boy here."

"You've got a very brave and resourceful son, Mr. McKinney," Hell said, accepting the rancher's handshake. The Ranger's grip was hard as horn, and as cool and dry as a snakeskin. "Not many boys his age would have had the gumption to do as he did."

"No, I reckon not," Hiram agreed, a hint of pride in his voice. "I'll be damned if I can figure out how you got into the house in the first place, though."

"I let him in, Pa!" Jake explained. "Miss Pretty Woman rode up this morning, while you was out tendin' the herd and Maw was out in the coop seein' to the chickens. She gave me this note that said Mr. Hell needed me to leave my bedroom window open so he could sneak in and hide before I went to bed. That way he could catch the haint unawares."

"Well, I'll be jiggered," Hiram said. "But, son—why didn't you tell your Maw and me what was goin' on?"

"I didn't think you'd believe me. Besides, I was afraid it might hurt y'all. I didn't want anything bad to happen to you and Maw on account of me."

Hiram looked into his son's face with a mixture of amazement, respect and love. "So you just kept goin' to bed, even though that thing was waitin' for you every night?"

"It weren't there *every* night. But, yes, sir, I did."

"Here you go, dear," Mrs. McKinney said, handing her husband a tin cup full of hot coffee. "How about you, Mr. Hell? Would could care for something to drink?"

"No thank you, ma'am," he replied, smiling without showing his teeth. "I don't drink—coffee."

Pretty Woman stepped out of Jake's room and coughed into her closed fist. Hell stood up, visibly relieved that he no longer had to make small talk.

"Ah! Pretty's finished with your unwanted guest. It's safe to go back in now."

"You sure?" Mrs. McKinney asked uneasily.

"Ma'am, there's not a lot of things in this world I'd bet good money on—but Pretty Woman's medicine is one of 'em."

As they entered the bedroom, the creature scuttled to the far corner, its head ducked low like that of a dog that's been kicked once too often. The speed of its movements made Mrs. McKinney cry out in alarm and clutch her husband's arm.

"No need to be fearful, ma'am," Hell said calmly. "The fight's been took out of it." He strode over to the creature and grabbed the grass-rope noose about its neck. "Come along, you," he snapped.

"What—what, exactly, is that thing?" Hiram asked, trying to keep the unease from his voice.

"I'm not rightly sure. I'll have to ask Pretty." Hell turned to the medicine woman and said something in Comanche.

The medicine woman wrinkled her nose as she replied in her native tongue, pointing to the walls as she spoke. Hell nodded his understanding.

"According to Pretty, this here's a nature spirit of some sort. These critters attach themselves to things like rocks, trees, creeks and the like—I reckon you could say they live in them. Some are friendly towards folks, others ain't. Seems this one attached itself to the tree that the planks used to build this room were milled from. By using various incantations and spells, in combination with a specially pre-pared rope, Pretty has rendered this particular spirit harmless—as long as y'all keep the noose about its neck, and feed it nothing but salt."

"Beg pardon?"

"Salt weakens unnatural things," Hell explained. "That is why the signs of power used in calling down the things from between worlds are drawn in salt; it saps their strength and binds them to the will of the conjurer." Hell stepped forward and handed the loose end of the rope to Jake. "I reckon he's yours, if he belongs to anyone. You'll find having your own private fiend has its advantages. For one thing, they chase off bad luck, as well as snakes. You feed this bogey a tablespoon of salt a day and he'll be yours until the oceans run dry and the mountains crumble. Provided you never take off the noose."

"What happens if it's removed?" Hiram asked, eyeing the creature cautiously.

"Just see that you don't," Hell replied gravely. "I don't do refunds."

After a few minutes of haggling, it was decided that five dollars cash money and a spool of ribbon was fair pay for a night of ghost-breaking. Though the McKinneys offered to let Sam Hell and Pretty

Woman spend the rest of the night in the barn, the pair politely declined.

"It is most kindly of y'all to extend such an invitation," the Ranger said, touching the brim of his hat. "But the nature of our business demands that we be on our way long before sun-up."

As they rode off into the night, Hell turned to look one last time at the McKinney clan as they stood in the dooryard of their homestead. Hiram leaned on his shotgun as he waved goodbye, his free arm draped over his wife's shoulders. Miriam McKinney stood close to her husband, occasionally casting worried looks in the direction of her son, who was busy poking the captive fiend in the rump with a sharp stick.

After they rounded a bend in the road and were no longer within line of sight of the McKinney ranch, Sam reached inside his duster and retrieved a long, thin cigar shaped like a twig.

"See? I told you advertising in the back of penny dreadfuls would pay off," he said, biting off the tip of the cigar with a set of very white, inhumanly sharp teeth.

"I'll grant you that," Pretty Woman replied in perfect English. "But I do not see how it will help you find the one you seek."

"Texas is a big place. I could wander forever and a day and never find him. But if something spooky is happening, odds are he might be near at hand. Kind of like high winds and hailstones mean a twister's nearby."

"There is something to your way of thinking," the medicine woman conceded. "But I still believe it was a waste of perfectly good money."

"I wouldn't say that. After all—you got yourself a nice spool of ribbon out of the deal, didn't you?"

"That thing could have torn me apart like fresh bread! That's hardly worth a spool of ribbon."

"But it didn't, did it? And that ribbon should look real nice wrapped around your braids."

"Point taken," she replied with a smile. "Still, do you think it was wise telling them so much about yourself?"

"I didn't let on too much. There was plenty of Rangers that fought at Rio Grande City and Brownsville. Besides, they don't know my real name. And there's no Rangers headquarters left to contact anymore, even if they did decide to try and check up on me. As far as the state of Texas is concerned, Ranger Sam Yoakum is long dead."

Chapter Three

Sam Yoakum first signed on with the Texas Rangers back in '58. Since then, he had fought more than his fair share of Comanche, Apache, Mexicans, cattle rustlers and outlaws, all for the grand sum of one dollar and twenty-five cents a day.

Now that Texas had joined the Confederacy, Yoakum knew it was only a matter of time before the Governor would be forced to muster what was left of the Rangers into an army, despite very real concerns that Cortina and Juarez would use the war between the gringo states to their advantage and attempt to reclaim Brownsville and the surrounding territory in the name of Mexico. But until the day he was expected to turn in his Ranger's star for a set of rebel grays, Yoakum continued to patrol his assigned territory and check on the various ranchers, settlers and townsfolk between Corpus Christi and the Rio Grande.

One such town was Golgotha, Texas—population forty-six, give or take a chicken or mule. Even from a distance, Yoakum could tell there was something not right about the place. Even the tiniest frontier settlement normally showed some sign of life, even if it was just a mangy dog wandering about or a horse tethered to a hitching post.

As he rode into Golgotha, the only things roaming the streets were tumbleweeds and dust devils.

The town was still. Not in the sense of it being a sleepy little village where nothing much happened, but in the way a dead body is utterly motionless. As the wind shifted in his direction, Yoakum caught the odor of spilled blood. During the Cortina War, when the Mexican bandit lord had laid waste to the lower Rio Grande Valley, Yoakum had come to know the smell of death all too well to ever mistake it for anything else.

He reined his mount to a halt before Haygood Swanson's General Mercantile. In his five years ranging the frontier, he had come to know the various townsfolk under his general protection fairly well. Goody Swanson, as he was known, was an affable fellow, who could be counted on for a free chaw and a decent price on salt, biscuits and coffee.

"Goody? Goody, are you there? It's Sam Yoakum!" His boot heels struck hollow notes on the raised boardwalk that fronted the store. As he pushed open the front door, the bell that alerted the shopkeeper that someone had entered his store gave a deceptively merry jingle.

The interior of Swanson's General Mercantile looked as if a tornado had hit it. Bolts of cloth lay strewn about the countertops, and the barrels that held the flour, sugar and nails lay on their sides, their respective contents spilled across the plank floorboards. Glass cases had been smashed, cabinets overturned and the pot-bellied stove that dominated the central room had been pulled free of its ventilation pipe and knocked onto its side. As he moved toward the back of the store, something crunched under his boot, and Yoakum smelled a cross between paint thinner and fermented grain. He glanced down and saw that he was walking through broken bottles of redeye.

Yoakum pushed his hat back and scratched his forehead, puzzled by what was before him. He didn't care how crazy they might be—Indians, outlaws and bandits never let whiskey—no matter how cheap—go to waste. If Cortina had raided the town, he would have taken every last barrel of flour he could have laid his hands on. After all, armies—even those comprised of bandits and outlaws—traveled on their stomachs.

As Yoakum turned to leave, something caught the corner of his eye. He bent over and picked up a shotgun from the tangle of unraveled cloth, broken glass and spilled sugar. The stock was marked with the initials h. s. and the barrel was bent back on itself. Yoakum dropped the useless weapon back where he found it and hastened out the door. He strode out into the middle of the empty street and cupped his hands to his mouth.

"*Hullo! Texas Rangers! Anybody here? Can anyone hear me?*" he shouted.

His only answer was the echo of his own voice. Whatever had happened to the citizens of Golgotha, it was more than a one-man job. He'd have to ride on down to Brownsville, pick up a couple of men and come back to sort things out.

Just as he was about to saddle up his horse, the tolling of a bell broke the eerie silence. Yoakum turned and looked in the direction of the sound. It was coming from the church, which stood in the very middle of town, catty-corner from the general store. The frantic nature of the bell ringing was more like a call for help than a somber call to prayers. He cast his gaze about, but saw no signs of life from any of the surrounding buildings.

He approached the whitewashed wooden church with his gun drawn, not knowing what to expect. As he drew closer, he could see several panes of stained glass had been busted out, as if by someone throwing rocks. The front door of the church swung inward as he touched it with the muzzle of his gun. As he stepped inside, a beam of sunlight illuminated the dim interior, falling across the figure of a solitary man, who stood at the back of the church, pulling on the bell rope that lead to the steeple.

"Where is everyone, Reverend?" Yoakum called out.

The bell-ringer stopped and turned to look at Yoakum. His face was gaunt and pale, covered with several days worth of gray stubble. His hair was greasy and uncombed, and his eyes were red-rimmed and more than a little wild, like those of a man who has stood guard on the ramparts with far too little sleep for far too long.

"I ain't no preacher," the bell-ringer replied. "And as for where everyone is—they're dead. Every last one of them. Ain't nothin' and no one left alive in Golgotha but me."

19

"And who might you be?"

"The name's Farley. I got me a place a couple miles east of town. I've been livin' in these parts since '52. You don't need to point a gun at me, Ranger," he said, nodding at Yoakum's pistol. "I ain't gonna give you no trouble."

"You say everyone's dead. If so, where are the bodies?"

"That's a long story," Farley said with a weary sigh.

"Humor me," he said, motioning for the other man to be seated in one of the nearby pews. As the other man sat down, Yoakum holstered his pistol but did not take his hand off its butt.

"It begun when Merle went and dug himself a new well. You see, he'd bought a parcel of land off this Meskin feller, name of Garcia. Merle already had him a place, but he wanted to build a little house on its own plot so he could bring his mama and the rest of his family down from Back East. He needed the new well, on account of the old one being too far away. Anyways, Garcia's old grandpa gets all riled up when he hears what Merle's doin'. He rides out and tells Merle he can't dig where he's diggin'.

"Merle tells him that he's bought the land off his kinfolk fair 'n' square, and if he wants to dig straight to hell, there ain't nothin' the old man can do about it. Then Old Man Garcia tells Merle that his grandson had no right to sell him the land without talkin' to him about it first. Merle says that's tough, but they've already signed papers on it and money has changed hands, so the sale is legal. Then Old Man Garcia offers to buy the land back from Merle—and at a good price, too. But Merle ain't havin' none of it. So Old Man Garcia, he goes home, packs up his family, and next thing you know they're gone—and they was in these parts since the conquistadors.

"After a few days diggin', Merle's about eight feet deep, I reckon. He's far enough down that he's got to use a ladder to get in and out of the hole. And he's got a couple of good ol' boys from town, Billy McAfee and Hank Pierson, out there helpin' him haul the dirt and rocks up topside. Then his spade strikes something made of metal, but it's too dark for him to see what it is.

"Merle yells up to Billy to lower him down some light. So Billy sends down a lantern. Merle lights it and bends over to get a look-see.

20

He finds what looks like the lid of a big iron box. There ain't much showin', but from what he can see it looks like it's the size of a steamer trunk. Merle and them get to talkin', and they decide that it must be buried treasure—maybe gold the Aztecs tried to hide from the Spanish, way back when. At first they mean to keep it to themselves, but as they get to uncoverin' the metal box, they realize it's too big and too heavy for just the three of them to pull it free of the hole.

"That's where I come in. I lived down the road a piece, and Merle knew I had me a string of mules. At first I didn't believe a word he said, but then he takes me over to where he's got the well started and tells me to climb down and take a look for myself. I have to admit that once they put the notion in my head, all I could think of was gold. I kept thinkin' that if that box was full of treasure, it would go a long ways to settlin' debts and makin' life easier for me an' mine. So I ran and fetched the mules and brought them back to the well.

"By this point, the boys had uncovered the whole damn thing. It was about four foot long, three foot high and three foot deep, with an old-fashioned hinged iron padlock. I hitched up the mules and wrapped the box in a set of chains I use to pull stumps. But when I laid my hand on the top of the box, I jumped back and hollered on account of it being so cold. My hand tingled and burned like I'd just stuck it in a bucket of ice water. Merle figgered it was cold like that because it had been buried so deep all them years. That didn't make much sense, but I was in too big a hurry to lay claim to my share of the treasure to give it much thought.

"I fastened the chains around the box and then climbed up top to fix them to the team. Usually my mules are pretty easy to work with, but that day they was givin' me fits, stompin' the ground and rollin' their eyes like they do when they smell somethin' fierce nearby, like a cougar or a bear. I really had to lay into them with the whip. Their rumps were runnin' red before they finally gave in and started to pull. But once they did, that ol' box was out of the bottom of Merle's well just as easy as yankin' a rotten tooth. Still, it took all four of us to lift it up and put it in the back of Merle's buckboard.

"By the time we finally managed to get the chest over to Merle's place, it was gettin' on dark. Since the danged thing was so heavy, we decided to just pull the buckboard into the barn and open it out there, as opposed to tryin' to drag it into the house. Billy and Hank rassled the bastard off the back of the wagon and set it on the barn floor.

"While Merle was busy fetchin' his chisel and pry-bar, I took a few seconds to study the padlock on the chest. It was a big rascal—as large as a baby's head—and when I looked at it close, I could make out some kind of symbols through the rust and the dirt caked on it. The funniest thing about the lock, I noticed, was it didn't have no keyhole. Once that critter was locked, it was meant to stay shut.

"Merle came back with the tools he needed to open the box, along with a lantern so he could see what he was doin' now that the sun was set. Merle weren't a small man, and he sure as hell weren't a weak one, but it took him several good swings with the hammer before he knocked that lock open. When it finally broke and dropped to the ground, we all stared at it for a couple of heartbeats, then looked up at one another. I don't know if it was the light from the lantern or somethin' else, but the other fellas seemed to be lit from inside with a terrible hunger that made their eyes burn like those of animals gathered around a campfire. I reckon I didn't look no different, though. Greed is a horrible thing.

"The lid of the chest was so heavy that Merle had to take the pry-bar and wedge it under the lip of the box. He levered it open enough so that Billy and Hank could grab hold and throw it all the way open. We crowded around, lantern held high, eager to sink our arms up to our elbows in gold coins and precious gems. But there weren't no treasure buried in that chest. Not by a long shot.

"The only thing the iron box contained was the body of a man lying on his side, knees drawn up and arms folded across his chest. 'Cept for a thin covering of yellowish, dry skin and wisps of hair that were still stuck to the scalp, it was basically a mummified skeleton. Going by the rusty breastplate and helmet it still wore, the dead man had once been a conquistador. The only thing of any possible value was a silver medallion set with a highly polished stone hung about its neck.

"Merle reached in and yanked the necklace free, holding it up to the light. Merle was always one for lookin' on the sunny side of things, so he tried to put a good face on it, so we wouldn't be so disappointed. 'At least it ain't a complete loss. This has to be worth at least fifty dollars . . .'

"That was the last thing I ever heard him say, at least that weren't screamin'.

"We all had our backs turned to the box, as we was lookin' over Merle's shoulder at the necklace he took off the Spaniard's carcass. Suddenly there was this cracklin' sound comin' from behind us, like someone walkin' through a pile of dead leaves. So I turn around, and I see—sweet Lord Jesus—I see the dead thing in the box stand up.

"I know what you're gonna say, now. That I must be crazy. But if I'm crazy, it's on account of what I seen in that barn. The thing that got out of the box weren't nothin' but bones with dry skin the color and texture of old leather stretched over 'em. But it still had eyes—or something like eyes—burnin' deep inside its sockets. And when the thing saw us, God help me, it grinned—peeling back black, withered lips to reveal a mouthful of sharp, yellow teeth.

"We was so flabbergasted we was froze to the spot, just like a covey of chicks hypnotized by a snake. I was too scared to swaller, much less scream. The dead thing, it made this noise like a screech owl and jumped on poor Merle. It sank its fangs into Merle's throat like a wolf takin' down a lamb. It sure as hell was spry for somethin' that had to have been dead three hundred years.

"Billy grabbed the thing and tried to rassle if off Merle, but it was like tryin' to pull off a tick. Even though it weren't but a bag of bones, it swatted Billy aside like he was nothin'. Hank snatched up an axe handle and laid into the thing, but just ended up splinterin' the handle on the iron breastplate it was wearin'. Still, he must have got its attention, cause it dropped Merle and turned on him instead.

"Things was happenin' and movin' too fast by this point for me to get a clear picture of what exactly was goin' on, but I remember that once the thing was finished with Merle, it didn't quite look the same. There seemed to be more meat on its bones, an' more juice in the meat. It was like the blood it had drained from Merle was fillin' its own veins.

"Billy starts screamin' 'It's got Hank! It's got Hank! We gotta save him!' He grabs up a pitchfork and charges th' thing, but it's too fast for him. It drops Hank and sidesteps Billy, snatchin' the pitchfork away like it was takin' a toy from a kid. Now Billy's screamin' for help, and—Lord, help me—instead of tryin' to save him, I ran away. I jumped on my horse and hightailed it to town, not lookin' back once for fear of what might be gainin' on me. Billy McAfee's death screams were echoin' in my ears the whole way.

"I reached Golgotha and I went straight to Sheriff Winthrop's office. He was in th' middle of dinner, so you can imagine he weren't too happy to have me bustin' in goin' on about dead things with glowin' red eyes murderin' Merle and them. Instead of ridin' out to check on my story, he just locked me up and told me to sleep it off.

"Now, I admit that I have been known to bend my elbow, and that I have been known to disturb the peace when I do, but that was no reason for Winthrop to simply ignore what I had to say. True, me and the boys had enjoyed a few celebratory shots of whiskey before we set to openin' the box, but I weren't drunk. Just like I ain't drunk now. Leastwise, not so drunk I was seein' things that weren't there.

"Anyhow, when I woke up the next day, I was still holdin' to my story. As Sheriff Winthrop was unlockin' my cell, I stuck my hand in my pocket and pulled out the medallion. During the ruckus, I must have snatched it up off the barn floor when Merle dropped it. Up until I pulled it out of my pocket, I'd forgot I even had it on me. I showed it to Winthrop as proof that what I was tellin' him was God's honest truth.

"I could tell he still weren't gonna swaller some long-dead conquistador risin' up from the grave and killin' folks, but the sight of the medallion made him wonder if there was something to my story. He decided to ride out to Merle's place and find out what was goin' on for himself. As for me, he told me to stay put in town, in case there was any questions that needed answerin' when he got back.

"I told him there was no way in hell I was goin' back out to my spread. Not with that thing, whatever it was, wanderin' the countryside. If he wanted to find me when he got back I told him I'd be in the church. The sheriff looked at me funny when I said that, because I ain't much for settin' foot in the Lord's house on a Sunday, much less any other day of the week.

"So I left the jail and come straight over here. The church was shut up, on account of it being the middle of the week, so I had to go get Brother Stephens, the minister here, to unlock it for me. The preacher, he was right surprised to see a sinner like me banging on his door. He asked me what I needed the church open for. I said I needed to do me some prayin'.

"He says, 'Well, that's mighty fine to hear, Farley. But you can pray to the Lord just as good at home.'

"But I tells him, 'Reverend, I got me some serious favors to be askin' of the Lord, and I figger its best I do my askin' on His ground, not mine.'

"He didn't rightly know what to make of my conversion, but I figger in the end he decided not to look it in the mouth. He went and unlocked the church and I set about praying as hard as I could, only lettin' up every so often to trot to the outhouse and back. Halfway into the afternoon, Sheriff Winthrop come back from Merle's spread. He tells Brother Stephens that he wants to talk to me some more, and would I come over to the sheriff's office. I tell the preacher to tell the sheriff that if he's got any questions to ask of me, he better ask them to me in the church, because I ain't settin' foot outside it. So Winthrop comes in and sits down in the pew next to me. I can tell from his face that he's worried some.

"'Farley,' he says, 'I been out to Merle's.'

"'You seen the well he was diggin'?'

"'I seen the well.'

"'You seen the barn?'

"'I seen that, too—as well as the metal chest you told me about.'

"'You seen Merle and them?'

"'No. That's the one thing I didn't see out there. There were no bodies in that barn. Hell, there weren't nothin', livin' or dead, in that barn. Not Merle, not Billy, not Hank—not even horses, for that matter.'

"'What does that mean, Sheriff?'

"'Damned if I know, Farley. Maybe you and Merle and the others had a fallin' out over the treasure in the chest. Maybe that's what happened. But it don't make no sense for you to come runnin' into town with such a cock-and-bull story if you kilt them. And why in tarnation would you want to kill Merle and his livestock, right down to the very last chick and piglet? And even if you did, why in hell would you hide the carcasses? Maybe you ain't tellin' me th' truth about what went on out there, but maybe you ain't lyin' to me, either. In any case, I have to wonder about what could possibly chase you so far up under Brother Stephens skirts. So until I get a better feel of what's goin' on here, I ain't gonna lock you up. I just want you to stay in town, where I can keep an eye on you.'

"I told him he needn't worry about that. I wasn't settin' foot outside the church unless I absolutely had to, since Brother Stephens said I could sleep in the vestibule until it was safe for me to go back home. The sheriff nodded and went back to his office.

"Things stayed quiet in Golgotha until the sun went down. That's when Merle and the boys showed up.

"The way I knowed they come back was the horse screamin' out in the street. I opened the door of the church and poked my head out and saw the three of 'em—Merle, Billy and Hank—swarming over the sheriff's palomino, which was hitched outside his office. They was all over it like cougars. At first I thought they was just loco, y'know? I called out to them to stop, more out of reflex, I reckon.

"They looked up from what they was doin' and I saw how pale they was—like there weren't a drop of life left in 'em. There was blood drippin' from their chins, and their eyes was all lit up from within, with the same hellfire I seen in the eyes of the thing from the box.

"Just then Sheriff Winthrop comes out to see what's happenin'. He's already got his gun drawn, not that it did him no good. The three of them jumped 'im just like they did his horse. Winthrop emptied most of his pistol into Merle, but he might as well have been shootin' at a tree. They took him down right then and there. That's when I slammed the church door and started prayin' again, even faster and harder than before.

"Folks poured out of their houses to see what all the shootin' and screamin' was about—and found out all too quick. At least half the town was kilt that night by them things. Brother Stephens rallied the other half and told 'em to make for the church. I reckon he knew creatures of the devil when he seen 'em, and knew they wouldn't be able to enter holy ground. Or maybe he thought it would be easier to make a stand in the church. I don't know which, because he didn't make it. He stopped to try and drag Martha Tillberry free of one of them monsters, and got his throat ripped out for his trouble.

"Us folks in the church couldn't do nothin' but listen to the creatures outside as they roamed the streets, laughing and shrieking like fiends from Hell. While they were able to enter other buildings freely, they wouldn't come closer than a stone's throw to the church. The reason I know this is because they was chuckin' rocks at us. They screamed and hissed like angry cats the whole time, too, like even lookin' in the direction of the church hurt 'em somehow. The rocks took out a couple of panes of glass, which is how we was able to keep an eye on them durin' that first night without openin' the door. It was horrible—there was bodies scattered all along the streets and boardwalks. Once or twice I caught sight of a tall figure moving between the buildings, the moonlight glinting off a metal vest and helmet.

"The next morning, when the sun finally came up, we looked back out the window and were surprised to see that the streets were completely empty. The bodies from the night before had vanished! It took a while, but we finally got the nerve to step outside and survey the damage. Except for the general store bein' turned ass over tea kettle and a few kicked-in doors and busted-out windows, there was little to show what had happened the night before—except for the lack of bodies. And it weren't just the townsfolk that was missin'. There weren't an animal carcass to be found—dog, cat, horse or pig. It was like everything that was livin' in Golgotha outside the protection of the church simply disappeared off the face of the earth.

"Those that survived the night were divided into two groups. There was them that wanted to get the hell out of town as fast as they could, and there was them that wanted to stay. Most of the folks that was for stayin' had loved ones missin'. I was one for stayin', but because I knew that without a horse, there was no way I could get far enough away before the sun went down. As bad as being holed up in the church might be, it was a damn sight better than bein' stuck out in the middle of nowhere with them things roamin' the countryside.

"The Wilhoyts and the Brubakers decided to pull up stakes and go. They took what provisions they could find from what was left of

Goody's store and loaded them up in a wheelbarrow. They struck out north. That's the way you come in, weren't it? You didn't pass them on the road, did you? There was nine of 'em—two men, two women and five young'uns."

Yoakum shook his head no.

"That's what I was skeered of. If them hell-beasts didn't git 'em, then Comanches or bandits most likely did. Either way, they're dead. Anyways, once the Wilhoyts and 'em was gone, that just left fifteen of us. We scavenged what we could from the store and houses—lamp oil, water, food, guns and ammunition—and went back to the church to wait for night.

"Soon as the sun was set, we could see things movin' outside. I watched as people—or what used to be people—wriggled their way out from under the boardwalks and dug themselves outta shallow graves. I watched as they wandered the streets of Golgotha, kinda dazed-like, as if they was all coming off the world's worst bender. They made this low, pitiful moanin' noise, like cattle lowing to be milked. They lifted their heads and started sniffing the air, like hounds casting for a scent. One by one they was drawn to the church, like iron filings to a magnet, but they couldn't get too close.

"It was terrible beyond any description. On the outside these were folks I'd worked alongside, broken bread with and called neighbor—folks like Goody Swanson, Tom Littlefield, Miz Tillberry—yet, they weren't them at all. One of the dead'uns came forward. It was Lottie Gruenwald, and she had dirt in her hair and dried blood all over her dress.

"'Oscar—where are you Oscar?' she calls out. 'I'm frightened!'

"Ol' Oscar jumped like he'd been stuck with a pitchfork when he heard her voice. 'That's my wife out there! She's in danger! She needs me!'

"I grabbed Oscar by the arm and tried to tell him that weren't his wife out there—leastwise, not anymore. But he wouldn't hear reason. He pushed me aside and ran right out the front door of the church to his lovin' wife—who put her cold, stiff arms around his neck and tore his throat out with her fangs. Funny thing is, he didn't scream or carry on, much less look scared. He kind of had this dreamy look on his face, even when she bit into him.

"Just as Lottie was startin' to drink Oscar's blood, there was a commotion among the others. Then this figure comes forward, partin' the crowd like Moses dividin' the Red Sea. It was him. The one from the box. The others started callin' his name, over and over, like children cryin' for their mama: '*Sangre, Sangre, Sangre.*'

"I tell you, it was enough to put a bald man's hair on end. As he got closer, I could see this Sangre's a damn sight improved from the first time I laid eyes on him. Except for his eyes and the pale color of his skin, he don't look that much different from any other feller you might meet on the street—'cept for the helmet and breastplate, of course. The moment Lottie saw him, she let Oscar drop to the ground, like a cat bringin' its owner a wounded mouse as a love-token.

"Now Oscar ain't dead yet, but he's gettin' there. He put one hand over his throat, the blood squirtin' between his fingers, and tried to drag himself back toward the church, but it was too late. This Sangre feller bent over and sank his teeth into Oscar's neck, worrying him like a terrier does a rat. Whatever spell Oscar was under must have been broken then, 'cause that's when he started screamin'. They don't last long, though. Once Sangre drunk his fill, he stepped back and the others closed in on the poor bastard, swarmin' him like ants on a lump of sugar.

"Despite what everyone in the church saw happen to Oscar, the same damn thing happened again and again that night. Husbands called to their wives, children called to their mothers, mothers called to their sons, brothers called to their sisters . . . It didn't seem to matter that steppin' outside was certain death. There was no talkin' sense into 'em. Even when a bunch of us knocked 'em down and sat on 'em to keep 'em from leavin', they would still find a way of gettin' out the door. By the time the sun rose, there was only six of us left, and half of them had become gibbering idjits.

"Once the streets was clear, we were finally able to get some sleep. Later that afternoon, those of us that were still in our right minds left to replenish our supply of water and food. When we returned, we found the ones we'd left behind hanging from the church rafters. There was nothing we could do but cut 'em down and place 'em outside, as it was too late in the day to try and bury 'em. That just left me, Cyrus Ledbetter and Joe Kelly.

"Once the sun went down, the dead'uns came back out from their hidey-holes and started fightin' with each other over the bodies we'd left outside. They got real violent about it, too—I seen what used to be Sheriff Winthrop rip the head off'n what used to be Hank. And Hank stayed dead that time. That tole me two things: that the pickin's had to be pretty slim, if they was scrappin' over corpse-blood, and that they could be killed—leastwise by one another.

"Their hunger made them more desperate, and they started movin' in closer on the church than they had the night before. It was plain to see that they was scared of comin' too close, but at the same time the pain in their bellies was making them bold. I guess starvin's the same, whether yore hankerin' for cornpone or human blood.

"Cyrus, Joe an' me decided it would be smart to sleep in shifts. That ways one of us would be awake to raise the alarm in case the dead'uns got a hair up their ass and decided to storm the church. Cyrus was to take the first watch, Joe the second and me the third. I bedded down the best I could, tryin' to tune out the sound of the dead'uns outside, moanin' and wailin' like the damned souls they were. Next thing I know, I wake up to find Cyrus on top of me, his hands wrapped around my throat.

"'It's you or me, Farley,' he growled. 'I already kilt Joe and fed 'im to 'em. Now its yore turn.'

"Cyrus should have checked to see if I was as harmless as Joe before trying to serve me up to those damned bloodsuckers. I reached into my boot and pulled out my knife and drove it into his belly. Needless to say, it weren't my cold bones the dead'uns ended up scrappin' over that night.

"That was two days ago. I been holed up here alone ever since. Every night they come back out, gettin' closer and closer to the church, like they're huddling around it for warmth. Last night they started fightin' amongst themselves something fierce—rippin' off haids and breakin' off arms and th' like.

"When I heard you hollerin', at first I thought I was dreamin'. When I looked out the window and saw you standin' out there in the middle of the street, I knew my prayers had been answered. I have been saved."

Yoakum took a deep breath and let it out slow. "Well, now, Farley . . . that's a mighty unusual story. I can honestly say that in all my years as a Texas Ranger, I have yet to hear tell of anything like it before—and I fought against Ironjacket and Cortina."

"I know it sounds like complete and utter horse hockey. But you have to believe me when I tell you every word of it is true. You want proof?" Farley thrust his hand into his pocket and withdrew a necklace attached to a pendant. "This here's the medallion Merle took off the dead'un in the box," he said, shoving the piece of jewelry into Yoakum's hand. "This is proof I ain't talkin' crazy, ain't it? You can have it, far as I care. All it brung me is misery."

Yoakum frowned at the pendant, turning it over in his hands. He moved to the broken stained glass window and held it up by its chain so that he could get a better look at the stone. He had never seen anything quite like it before. Depending on its angle, it appeared black, while other times it seemed to glow red as a ruby. He was so preoccupied staring into the stone's depths, he did not realize that Farley was behind him until a gun butt collided with the back of his head.

Chapter Four

WHEN YOAKUM CAME TO, it was to find himself alone. Late afternoon shadows filled the church. As he got to his feet, he grimaced and gingerly touched his skull. His fingers came away sticky with blood. He lurched out into the dying light of the setting sun. There was no sign of either his horse or Farley.

"Goddamn lyin' horse thief," he muttered under his breath. All that bastard had left him was a piece of junk jewelry, tucked inside the front breast pocket of his shirt, and the grandpappy of all headaches. But as he stood in the deserted street, Yoakum could not help but remember Farley's story about the living dead. It was pure poppycock, plain and simple—it had to be. But if Farley had been lying, then where had everybody gone?

As the Texas sun dropped its blood red eye, and the lengthening shadows drew the town into dusk, Yoakum heard what sounded like a dog pawing at a door. As he turned around, trying to pinpoint the source of the noise, he realized that the sound was coming from more than one place. The scratching was quickly replaced by a louder, more distinct noise—one that made every hair on the back of his neck stand on end. It was a chorus of human voices, united in an ululating wail of pain and despair. It was the cry of the dead'uns.

He saw the first one crawl out from under the shadows of the boardwalk, pulling itself along on its elbows like a Comanche brave sneaking up on a buffalo. The creature was covered from head to toe in a mixture of dirt, manure and mud, although there were enough clean spots for Yoakum to see that the flesh underneath was as pale as death. Its eyes locked onto him shining with an unwholesome hunger. It took an active force of will for the ranger to tear himself from the thing's gaze.

To his horror, there were dozens of similar creatures boiling out from under the boardwalks and crawlspaces of the surrounding buildings, like maggots escaping a corpse. He made a mental note to himself to amend his opinion of Farley. The man was definitely a horse thief, but he certainly wasn't a liar.

He turned to flee to the relative safety of the church, only to find his way blocked by more of the erstwhile citizens of Golgotha. They stood shoulder to shoulder, their bloodless faces fixed into masks of depraved longing. He'd rescued men held captive by Indians until they where starved into scarecrows who didn't look that hungry. He fired his Colt .45 into the crowd that encircled him. Of the six dead'uns he hit, only one dropped and stayed down—from a head wound that took off her sunbonnet along with the top of her skull.

With a collective shout of anticipation, the creatures surged forward, clawing at Yoakum with yellowed nails. They swarmed over him like rats attacking a wounded terrier, violently biting and clawing one another as they jockeyed for position. Yoakum kicked, punched, bit and gouged eyes as best he could, but they seemed immune to any punishment he meted out. In the end, there were simply too many of them. Within seconds of emptying his pistol, he was overwhelmed.

What had once been the town's blacksmith clamped cold, clammy fingers about Yoakum's throat. The Texas Ranger drove his fist into the undead thing's face with all his might. Though he could feel the creature's jaw break from the force of the blow, his attacker continued to pull him inexorably forward. As the blacksmith opened his mouth, a graveyard stench rolled forth, causing Yoakum to gag. He didn't know what was worse—dying at the hands of fiends, or having to endure their stink while doing it. Suddenly, there was a shout that froze the entire congregation in their tracks.

"¡La Parada!"

The dead'uns crowded about Yoakum abruptly withdrew. As the burly blacksmith let go of Yoakum's throat, the Ranger dropped to his knees, coughing raggedly as he fought to regain his breath. He looked up as he massaged his bruised and swollen neck, staring in mute amazement at the figure before him. Even if he had not heard Farley's story about the mummified conquistador, he still would have known that this was their leader, the one they called Sangre.

The Spaniard stood well over six feet tall, with long black hair that fell past his shoulders, and an equally dark beard and goatee that gave his face an appropriately saturnine appearance. Save for his pallid complexion and a set of overlong, yellowed fingernails, there was little to indicate to the casual observer that he was as cold as yesterday's mutton.

Sangre stared down at Yoakum with eyes that glittered like rubies held before a flame. Although he still wore the rusty *morion* helmet and armored vest he had originally been buried in, the revived conquistador was also outfitted in a pair of denim trousers and cowboy boots, no doubt taken from one of his recent victims. The others milled about him at a respectful distance. The way they kept their eyes riveted on him, while avoiding his gaze, reminded Yoakum of a pack of hounds anxiously awaiting their master's command.

The undead conquistador pointed a talon-like finger at Yoakum and spoke in a booming voice. "¡Primero sangres es mía!"

The dead'uns muttered to themselves. It was clear that they did not like what Sangre had to say, but were unwilling to argue the matter. The conquistador allowed himself a smile, displaying fangs the color of antique ivory.

"*La paciencia, mis niños. Después que yo soy hecho, èl es suyo.*"

"Like hell!" Yoakum growled, spitting a wad of bloody phlegm onto the conquistador's boots. Like most Texans, he understood Spanish about as well as he did English. And he knew he didn't like what he was hearing, no matter what the language. "I ain't no side of beef to be parceled out amongst your kin!"

Sangre grabbed the Ranger by the front of his shirt as if he weighed no more than a child. As Yoakum looked directly into Sangre's burning red eyes, he heard a voice that was not his own murmuring inside his head, urging him to stop struggling and surrender. He felt a sudden pressure on his throat, immediately followed by a piercing pain. Within seconds of being bitten, the wound went numb, as if a paralyzing toxin had been injected into his system. He felt as if he were somehow standing outside his own body, watching as he struggled to escape.

Summoning the last of his strength, Yoakum pulled himself away from the conquistador. Sangre responded by tightening his grip. There was a tearing sound, and the pocket of Yoakum's shirt came away in Sanger's hand. The medallion in his pocket fell to the ground between them. The Spaniard yowled as if Yoakum was hot to the touch, and quickly distanced himself from the wounded Ranger.

"¡Recoja ese *collar de Diablo!*" Sangre snarled, pointing at the medallion at his feet as if it were a rattlesnake coiled to strike. The dead'uns shuffled their feet and eyed the amulet cautiously. None moved forward to retrieve it. "¡Lo toma lejos!" the conquistador thundered.

Yoakum snatched up the medallion and swung it in a wide arc, turning to face the others as they crowded in. The creatures moved back, parting before him like the Red Sea. Yoakum realized he could either go back into the church, or he could strike out on foot. Either way, he'd be dead before dawn. But better that he die under the open sky than holed up somewhere with his back to the wall, like a baited bear.

Yoakum half expected the creatures to dog-pile him the moment his back was turned, but they simply stood by and allowed him to walk away. It was clear from the hungry looks they gave him they wanted nothing more than to tear into him like a Sunday dinner, but something was holding them back—and that something was the mysterious pendant he held in his hands.

Within minutes he was outside the city limits of Golgotha. He had never been so happy to put a town behind him in his life. The relief he felt upon escaping, however, was quickly replaced with concern. As usual, he was out of the frying pan and into the fire. He was a white man wandering alone, wounded and unarmed in the most hostile territory in Texas. He had no food or water, and nothing more than the clothes on his back to protect him against the elements. It was dark, and he had nothing to light his way but the rising moon and the evening stars.

Once he was convinced that Sangre and his followers were not coming after him, he slipped the amulet around his neck and turned his attention to the bite on his throat. Though it was not particularly deep, it continued to bleed long after it normally should have clotted. He was able to temporarily staunch the wound by wrapping it with his bandana, but it was not long before the cloth was saturated. He was weary from walking and becoming increasingly lightheaded, but he knew better than to stop and rest. Even if Sangre's whey-faced spawn weren't after him, odds were the smell of his blood would attract any number of predators. The last thing he needed in such a weakened condition was to find himself face to face with a mountain lion or a pack of coyotes. Hell, the way he was feeling, he wouldn't be able to lick a prairie dog.

As he continued walking, he became dimly aware that he was no longer traveling alone. There was a figure keeping pace with him, one that he could only see from the corner of his eye. The figure was that of a man, dressed in overalls and heavy boots, and he carried a chopping hoe in his left hand, which he used as a walking staff. Though Yoakum could not immediately place the stranger, there was something familiar about him. Then the man turned his head and smiled at him, and, with a start, Yoakum realized he was looking into the face of his father.

"Daddy?"

"Best be careful, son," Silas Yoakum said. He extended his right hand, in the palm of which was the severed head of a rattlesnake. "They can still bite after they're dead."

The elder Yoakum smiled and quickly closed his fist about the viper. As he did so, his features began to rapidly swell and turn purple, the eyes bulging from their sockets, until he looked like he did the last time his son had seen him, twenty years ago.

Sam had been working the fields, chopping cotton, when he heard his father cry out in pain and anger. As he hurried to his father's side, he saw Silas Yoakum's arms rise and fall numerous times, swinging the hoe he carried down onto something near his feet. By the time Sam reached him, Silas had chopped the rattlesnake into ribbons. The older man waved his ten-year-old son away.

'Go fetch your Maw,' he rasped. Those were the last words Silas Yoakum ever spoke.

Suddenly Sam was back at the house, sitting in the kitchen at his place at the table. The stove must have been on, because the room was hot. Yoakum heard the door open, and he turned to see his mother enter the house, holding out her apron, which was full of blue bonnets from the pasture.

"Aren't they lovely, Sam?" she asked. "They're dead but they still look like they're alive. Mercy, it's so hot in this kitchen! They'll need to drink if they are going to keep looking lively. They're dead, but they can still be thirsty. Be a good boy and draw me some water."

"Yes, ma'am," he replied, dutifully walking across the kitchen to the sink. He had to give the kitchen pump handle a couple of good pushes before the water spurted forth. As he watched the cold, clear spring water splash into the waiting catch basin, he was suddenly aware of just how hot and thirsty he was.

He leaned forward and placed his lips against the spout, eager to drink his fill. To his surprise, the water was not cool and refreshing, but warm and slightly salty. He drew back and saw that it was not well-water spurting forth, but blood. Even as he retched, something in the back of his mind urged him to continue drinking from the gushing gore. Though he knew he should resist the urge, he was helpless to fight it. It was as if his body was being devoured from the inside out by a ferocious heat, which could only be slaked by the blood of others.

As Yoakum fought against the dark fire burning inside him, he became dimly aware of what felt like a soothing, feminine hand on his fevered brow, accompanied by a slowly expanding numbness. The numbness overwhelmed the hellfire within his veins, dampening it to a tolerable level, if not exactly extinguishing it altogether. As the lack of sensation spread throughout his body, he wondered if he was dying.

The idea did not bother him overmuch. Better to die a man than to live as a monster.

The next thing he was aware of was the smell of wood smoke and the sound of a woman's voice, chanting in a language he recognized as belonging to the Comanche. It took him a moment to realize he did not need to open his eyes because they were already open, staring at what looked to be the backside of a horse blanket. He reached up and pulled it away, and found himself gazing up at the night sky.

As he sat up, he saw the source of both the smoke and chanting. An Indian woman dressed in buckskin riding trousers hunkered before a small campfire, her back to him. Her hair was long and hung down her back like the mane of a wild pony. Upon hearing him move, she turned her head to look at him, and he could see she was naked from the waist up, save for a beaded pectoral and the paint on her face.

"Who are you?" he rasped, his voice drier than ginned cotton. When the woman did not respond, he asked the question haltingly in her own language.

"I will speak in your own tongue," she replied. "Your Comanche hurts my ears. I am called Pretty Woman."

"How long have I been asleep?"

"You have been dead three days."

"You mean unconscious."

She gave him a look that would wither an apple on the branch. "I know dead when I see it."

"How can I be dead if I am talking to you?"

"How can a rattlesnake bite after it is no longer alive?"

Yoakum blinked. "I had a dream where someone said that to me. But how—?"

Pretty Woman shrugged her shoulders and went back to poking at the fire with a stick. "Dreams tell us many things. My dream told me where to find you, and to protect you from the sun."

"I don't understand."

"I don't, either. For now it is enough that I saw you in my dream and found you before you burned with the rising sun."

"And you sat with me this whole time? Three days?"

"Yes."

"Why?"

"I am a shaman. As was my grandfather and his mother before him. My medicine is strong, but I am still young. I am—unseasoned," she spoke in a way that told Yoakum she was quoting someone else's words. "So I was sent out into the wilderness to seek a vision, and make its medicine my own.

"For four days and four nights I wandered without food or drink, or sleep. Then, on the fifth night, I looked up and saw the moon weeping blood. The bloody teardrops fell upon the land, and from them sprang forth a man with eyes of fire and the heart of a devil. I saw the devil-man go forth and bring pestilence and death to the Whites and the Mexicans, and to my people as well. I saw towns and villages laid to waste, filled with the dead who are not dead. I saw the fire that burned in the devil-man's eyes glowing in the eyes of all those he tainted— including my own kin.

"The vision frightened me beyond any fear I have ever known. I looked back to the moon for guidance, but it was no longer there. In its place was a man whose face was whiter than a cloud, and whose eyes blazed red, but not with the same fire that burns within the devil-man. That face was yours."

"The devil-man you saw in your vision—he is real. His name is Sangre." He put his hand to his throat, a baffled look on his face. "But if I am, indeed, dead—how is it I still have my wits about me? I've seen what happens to those he bites. They're little more than animals, driven by the need for blood."

"The charm you wear protects you," Pretty Woman said, pointing at the medallion still looped about his neck. "I do not know the medicine that worked it, but it is very old and very strong."

He looked down at the pendant hanging against his chest, taking the stone in the palm of his hand. His flesh tingled and burned for a few seconds, as if reacting to the silver, before the pain was replaced by a familiar numbness. Where the stone had previously appeared red laced with skeins of black, now it resembled a glass filled with red and black ink that swirled together, yet never mixed.

"All I know about this necklace is that Sangre had it on him when he was found, and he didn't come back to life until it was removed. And I know that he, and the others like him, are scared of it."

"Ah!" Pretty Woman said, nodding her head as if it all suddenly made sense. "It is a containment charm. Its medicine holds and binds evil spirits that dwell within the flesh of the walking dead. It has placed the demon inside you under a spell, so it can not control your flesh."

"What would happen if I took it off?"

"The evil spirits would be free to do as they like."

"I have to go back to the place where this all began. It's my job to ride the range and deal with those situations the local law can't handle. I've got to go back and see to it that Sangre doesn't do to the rest of Texas what he did to Golgotha. That son of a bitch started shit on my watch, in my territory—I'll be damned if I ain't the one who's gonna stop it."

"Do you think that's wise? You don't even know if you have the power to stop this Sangre."

"I've always done my duty by going where I was needed, no matter what the circumstances, whether it was riding down rustlers, hunting banditos or fighting redskins—no offense, ma'am. I don't see why I should stop now."

"I know the place of which you speak. It is a half-day's ride from here—if we had horses. Besides, you can not travel during the daylight hours."

"Who said anything about we? I'm the one who has to go, not you. Besides, it will be far more dangerous after dark for you than it will be for me."

"I have ways of protecting myself against such creatures," Pretty Woman replied. "Besides, this is part of my quest. I not only saw you in my vision, but the one you call Sangre as well. That means our destinies are intertwined."

He dropped his shoulders in resignation. He could tell there was no talking her out of it. And, truth to tell, part of him did not want to strike out alone. They walked for the rest of that night, before holing up in an outcropping of rock that provided enough shade to wait out the daylight. Upon the setting of the sun, they resumed their march. It was close to midnight by the time they reached the outskirts of the town.

Sam frowned and paused, tilting his head. "He's gone," he said flatly.

"How do you know?"

"I'm not sure. It's like the hairs going up on the back of your neck when you know you're close to something dangerous. You just feel it—or, in this case, I don't feel him."

It had been just over three days since Yoakum had last been in Golgotha, but the town was almost unrecognizable. Save for the church and the general store, every building had been burned to the ground. Among the still-smoldering timbers were a number of bodies covered in soot and ash, their limbs contorted and scorched.

"What happened here?" Pretty Woman asked in a hushed voice as they surveyed the carnage.

"I'm not sure," Yoakum replied. He scanned what was left of the town, trying to apply his lawman's knowledge to an outlaw beyond human experience. "Lord knows I've seen more than my fair share of massacres, but nothing like this! Whatever happened, it looks as if they did this to themselves. It's as if they were winnowing themselves out.

"And if Sangre isn't here—where is he? I know for a fact that there wasn't a living pack animal for twenty miles in any direction. If he did leave on foot, how could he do so without the risk of exposing himself to sunlight?"

He fell silent as his gaze fell on the town cemetery, located behind the church. Cursing under his breath, he motioned for Pretty Woman to follow him. As they drew closer, Sam could see that a number of the graves had been desecrated, the bodies pulled from their final resting places and tossed about like so many macabre dolls.

"There are thirteen open graves and thirteen missing caskets," the Ranger said. "That means, of the forty-plus people that lived in Golgotha, only twelve are left, plus Sangre. Judging by these tracks, they all headed out on foot, taking their coffins with them. That way they can travel by night and are guaranteed a place to hide from the sun during the day. These drag marks show them heading in every direction of the compass. And there's no way for me to know which track belongs to Sangre.

"Merciful God, it's like when a ship runs aground and all the rats in the hold swarm out before anyone can discover the crew is dead of the plague. How can I possibly stop this from spreading across the country? I'm just one man."

As he stared out into the vast emptiness of the Texas wilderness, a sense of hopelessness rose within him. During his life he had never known such feelings, even after his father died. He had been faced with ruthless enemies and impossible odds before, but back then he had been part of a larger organization. If he could not handle a situation on his own, he knew there were other Rangers he could call on to back him up. But that was all gone now, sucked into the same void that had claimed his life.

There was a touch on his shoulder as light as a butterfly's. He turned to find Pretty Woman standing beside him. As she brushed back the hair from her face, he realized for the first time how true her name was.

"You are wrong about two things, Sam. You are no longer a man. And you are not alone."

Chapter Five

TEXAS, 1869, ONCE MORE:
The sun was down. Yoakum knew this because he was able to move once more. Over the years, he had developed a means of surviving as a creature of the night in a land of relentless sunshine. Every morning, just before the dawn, he would crawl into his custom-made shroud of canvas, secured on the inside by leather laces set in metal gussets. Then Pretty Woman would sling the shroud—with him inside—over the back of his horse, so that they could continue to travel. Upon growing tired, she would find an appropriate spot to make camp. Once dusk had settled, he would awake and once more resume his semblance of life.

One of the first things Yoakum had learned upon becoming a dead'un was that despite his superhuman strength and relative immunity to physical harm, it was difficult for a dead'un to survive in the world of the living without the help of humans. He knew for a fact that he would never have survived to see his first night as a dead'un, much less his first year, if not for Pretty Woman's intervention. After all, it was she who guarded his shroud while he slept. She was the one who handled buying feed for their horses, dealing with tradesmen and other such mundane business situations that required someone able to travel about in the daylight.

Indeed, three of the original twelve Golgotha dead'uns had perished within their first week. The first had made the mistake of attempting to ford a river, unaware that running water renders dead'uns immobile. The current quickly separated the dead'un from the coffin he was carrying, sending both spinning downriver, where the casket was dashed to bits on the rocks while the creature was snared by the branches of a partially submerged tree. The dead'un remained trapped, helpless to free himself, until the sun rose. Sam and Pretty Woman found what was left of him the next evening, still entangled in the deadfall's embrace.

The second dead'un had managed to find a small cave in the foothills, where he hid in his coffin during the day. However, while he was asleep, a pack of coyotes that usually made the cave their home dragged his carcass out of the casket and devoured it. When Hell arrived, he found a pup busily gnawing away at the creature's skull as if it were a ball.

The third dead'un had more sense when it came to finding a place to hide her casket, choosing the hayloft of an old barn. However, her fatal mistake was that she lost track of time while out hunting. As the sun began to rise, her long, unbound hair caught fire. As she fled back to the safety of her coffin, her hair trailing behind her like a blazing bridal veil, she ignited the surrounding bales of hay, burning the entire structure to the ground, herself along with it.

The rest of the dead'uns spawned from the Golgotha massacre, however, proved far better at survival than those three. Over the last few years, with Pretty Woman's help, of course, he had succeeded in tracking down and exterminating the remaining nine, as well as their own unholy spawn.

While Yoakum had put his skills as a tracker to good use in hunting each of them down, what he relied on the most was a kind of sixth sense he acquired after being bitten. Whenever there was anything supernatural within a certain radius, he could feel it drawing him forward, like a magnet attracts a piece of iron. The closer he was to something of the supernatural world, the more intense the pull became. In the years he had spent hunting monsters, it had yet to let him down. And now he was feeling the persistent tug of the paranormal yet again, like an angler with a fish gently nibbling on his line.

"There's something out there," he said. "I can feel it."

Pretty grunted and tossed what was left of the coffee onto the campfire. "Can you tell what it is?"

"Not yet," he replied with a shake of his head. "Might be a ghost. Could be something more tangible. Hard to tell. I need to get closer before I can draw a bead on it."

"What direction?"

"Thataway," he said, pointing west.

The McKinney's ranch and the gently rolling rangelands of the Lower Rio Grande Valley had long since given way to the less forgiving landscape of Western Texas. Upon crossing the Pecos River, the flatlands were replaced by the mountains that marked the boundary between the Great Plains and the Cordillera. They were now in the high desert, where the lowlands and highlands were equally bare of trees, and where only the highest mountain peaks supported stunted forest growth.

They had been following the pull for the better part of a week when they finally made the crest of a rise, and Hell found himself looking down at surprisingly familiar surroundings.

"I know this place. At least I used to, back during my Ranger days," he said as he stared down at a large, two-story house surrounded by several smaller outbuildings. "It's called Tucker's Station. It's a trading post that doubles as a way station for the San Antonio-San Diego stage route. Fella name of Jimbo Tucker runs this place, along with his wife, Dottie. Decent folks, if memory serves."

"Do they know you?"

"I only met them once or twice, and that was before the war. Odds are they wouldn't recognize me. Besides, there's always the chance they've moved on and someone else is running things now."

"Do you want to risk it?"

"We'll have to. Whatever I've got a line on has been here recently. I can feel it." As they approached the trading post, Hell pulled the reins in on his horse, bringing it to a sudden halt. "You hear that?" he whispered.

"I don't hear anything."

"That's just it. It's *too* quiet. The Tuckers had themselves a big ol' coonhound that would howl like the dickens the moment anyone rode in. And even at this time of night, we should be able to hear the livestock making some kind of noise. I've only been one other place that was as quiet as this place is right now—Golgotha."

Hell dismounted, signaling for Pretty Woman to do the same. They approached the main building from opposing sides, moving fast and low, weapons drawn. Pretty Woman circled around back while Hell approached the front. No lamplight came from any of the windows facing the dooryard. None of the curtains so much as twitched. As Hell approached the front door, he caught a stench so foul it made him stagger.

"Hold it right there!" a voice called out from the deep shadow cast by the wooden overhang suspended above the door.

"One step closer and I'll blow your ass to Kingdom Come!"

"I mean no harm, friend," Hell replied, holstering his gun.

The owner of the voice stepped forward, revealing himself to be a man in his late fifties, with unkempt gray hair and whiskers. The old-timer had the wiry build and sunburned skin of a veteran fence-rider, dressed in a denim work shirt and well-worn dungarees. He was also armed with a shotgun, which was pointed level at Sam's chest. As the older man moved closer, favoring his left leg, the stink moved along with him.

"Who the heck are you, stranger?" the old-timer asked.

"The name's Hell. Sam Hell," he replied, coughing into a clenched fist. "What is that stink?"

The muzzle of the shotgun wavered slightly. "Afraid that's me," he explained, gesturing to his pants, which were soaked from the knees down in shit. "Now what do you want, mister?"

"I want you to put down your shotgun."

"I'm afraid that just ain't gonna fuckin' happen."

"Want to put money on that, old man?" Pretty Woman asked as she reached around the old-timer's shoulder and placed the blade of her knife against his grizzled throat.

"Let's not do anything god-damn rash," the old man said as he dropped the shotgun and put his hands on the top of his head. "Pardon, my French."

"You have nothing to fear from us. As I said, my name is Sam Hell, and this is my traveling companion, Pretty Woman."

The old-timer raised an eyebrow and let out with a low whistle. "My-my! Ain't you as fine as cream gravy, even if you is a squaw."

"I could have slit your throat from ear to ear, you old buzzard," Pretty Woman growled in reply as she returned her knife to its sheath. "Don't make me regret that."

"A feisty one, eh?" he grinned, displaying missing teeth.

Pretty Woman rolled her eyes and turned to address her traveling companion. "I checked the back way. No sign of life. Even the pigs in the sty are gone."

Hell fixed the old man with a hard stare. "Okay, mister—?"

"Johnson. But most folks call me Cuss."

"All right, Cuss—where is everybody?"

"They're gone. Carried off by a bunch of cocksucking fiends. Pardon my French."

"Come again?"

"You wouldn't believe my story, even if I told you."

"You'd be surprised by what I'll believe," Hell replied, pulling a handkerchief from his back pocket and placing it over his nose. "But would it be too much of a bother for you to change out of those clothes before you start telling it?"

In deference to Sam and Pretty Woman's olfactory senses, Cuss lead them to a small shed near the livery stable that served as his living quarters. The interior was spartan, but surprisingly tidy, with the only furniture being a rope bed fitted with a horsehair mattress, a chair and small washstand with a basin.

"Normally, I'm a modest man," the ranch hand said as he reached under his bed and dragged out a pasteboard suitcase. "I don't usually change my drawers in front of them who ain't kin, or at least I haven't rode with a spell. But modesty be damned! I can't stand myself any longer!"

Cuss removed a folded pair of dungarees from the suitcase and snapped them open with a practiced flick of his wrists. He kicked off his boots and unbuttoned the fly of his soiled jeans, peeled them off and tossed them out the front door. Dressed in nothing but his union suit, he sat down in the solitary chair and began to pull on his clean pants.

"Aren't you gonna change your long johns, too?" Hell asked.

"Ain't got but one god-damn pair," Cuss grunted as he threaded a belt through the loops of his pants. "Besides, they been through worse without needin' a wash."

"Maybe you could borrow a pair from the Tucker's inventory? I'm sure they wouldn't mind."

"I already checked the trading post," Cuss sighed, wiping at the muck that encrusted his boots with an old rag. "Them thievin' marauders took everything that weren't nailed down. Pots, pans, blankets, bolts of trade cloth . . . you name it, they hauled it off."

"You want to tell us what happened?" Hell asked, folding his arms across his chest.

The ranch hand stared at the boot he held in his hands for a long moment before replying. "I been workin' for the Tuckers ever since I got throwed by that god-damn bronco over at the Lazy J. Must be goin' on five years now. It busted up my leg somethin' awful. Doc said I was lucky they didn't take it off at the knee. It's good for walkin' and such, but it keeps me from ridin' herd. Jimbo, he took me on after that. Mostly I see to the horses, while him and the missus tend to the folks that come through. The pay ain't much, but I got a clean, dry place to bunk, and I'm allowed to take my meals in the house. For an ornery ol' hoot-owl like myself, I have to say it's a sweet deal.

"We don't get much in the way of trouble out here. The stage comes and goes twice a week, and that's about it in terms of excitement. The Tuckers have made a point of bein' fair in their dealings, and it's helped keep them in good stead with the Injuns and Meskins hereabouts. The worst we've ever had to worry about was a horse thief or two. But that was before today.

"I knowed there wasn't something right with them cocksuckers the moment I clapped eyes on 'em. There was ten of 'em: eight men and two women. They was drivin' three covered wagons. Claimed they was homesteaders headed out West. They said they'd been on the road for the better part of a month and were runnin' low on flour and sugar and the like, and were hankerin' to spend a night under a solid roof. But they didn't strike me as settlers. For one, the men seemed a touch hard for farmers, if you get my drift. The womenfolk didn't strike me as proper ladies, neither. And there weren't a young'un to be seen, which struck me as odd. Besides, I don't trust folks that smile when they ain't got no god damn reason to, and these folks was showin' way too much teeth for my liking.

"I ain't the most sociable of fellers, but Jimbo, he's a natural-born host. Always happy to see folks, eager listen to their stories and do whatever it takes to sell 'em whatever they need before sendin' them on their way. He told me to go make sure their horses were properly stabled. So I go to unhitch their horses and put 'em up in the barn, so they can get watered and fed, right? But one of 'em comes runnin' up and says he'll tend to it himself. It weren't no skin off my nose, but it struck me as peculiar. I couldn't help but feel like maybe there was somethin' in them wagons they didn't want me to know about. But all I saw in the first wagon was a long wooden box, like them cedar chests you keep blankets in.

"I told Jimbo I thought maybe the newcomers might be gunrunners lookin' to deal with the Apache, but he said I was bein' suspicious and unchristian. Suspicious, hell!" Cuss said with a bitter laugh as he spat on the boot he was cleaning. "I'm just cautious is all. Anyways, just before dusk, the El Paso stage pulls up, more or less on time. Besides the driver, Clem Jones, and his assistant Elmer, there was an older married couple name of Crocker and some flannel-mouthed salesman out of St. Louis, which meant that the station was gonna be packed to the rafters come suppertime.

"Like I said, normally I take my meals at the Tucker's table, but the idea of breaking bread with those homesteaders didn't sit right with me. So when Jimbo told me that there weren't no room for me, on account of the guests, I weren't sore about it. Dottie still fixed me up a plate of fried chicken and cat-head biscuits, smothered in white-eye gravy, and had her youngest, Loretta, run it out to me, along with a jar of sassafras tea.

"After I was finished with my feed, I fetched my pipe and tobacco so's to have my evening smoke before turnin' in. The sun had only been down about five minutes when I heard screams comin' from the house. I look out my door and see lit'l Loretta run out, two of the homesteaders hot on her heels. Seein' how she's a wee thing, and they was big, strong cocksuckers, it didn't take much for 'em to tackle her and drag her back indoors. I grabbed my shotgun, snuck up on the house and looked in the window to see what was going on.

"Them god-damn phony homesteaders had Jimbo and the others lyin' on the floor, trussed up like turkeys ready for a shoot. Then in walked this tall drink of water I ain't seen before. He was dressed in a fancy-ass embroidered silk vest with smoked glass cheaters, like a high-card gambler. By the way the others kowtowed to him, I could see he was the boss of the outfit.

"At first I figgered he must have rode in from wherever it was he'd been hidin' during the day, but there weren't a spot of dust on him. I wondered where this feller had been keepin' himself, if he'd been at the station all along without me seein' him. Then he smiled, and I seen his teeth, and I remembered the wooden box in the back of the wagon.

"I ain't an educated man, but I ain't no god-damn fool. I don't normally hold with superstition. But I been around the barn more than once, and I seen things in my day there weren't no way of explainin'. And what I saw through that window was the Devil made flesh, and there's no way anyone can tell me fuckin' different.

"The boss-devil, he snatched up Jimbo off the floor and tossed him onto the table like he was a Sunday ham. Then he buried his fangs in his throat and drank his blood like a hound lappin' up buttermilk. When I saw that, I couldn't help but call out to Jesus. The boss-devil, he yanked his head up and stared right at where I was hidin' and pointed a finger in my direction. The nails on his hands were as long and yellow as the claws on a buzzard.

"I knew there was no way I could outrun 'em with my bum leg, even with a head start. I had to hide, and hide quick. The closest place was the jakes. I pulled the door shut just as the boss-devil's posse poured out of the house, runnin' here and there, checkin' the barn, sheds and other buildings. I could tell they weren't gonna stop lookin' until they found me.

"What I did next was the only thing I *could* do if I wanted to survive—I lifted up the privy box and crawled down the goddamn hole. Lucky for me, it was a relatively new crapper—Jimbo and me had dug it just a month before—so I was only standing in muck up to my knees, not my chin. As bad as I smell now, it ain't *nothin'* compared to the stench down there!

"I'd just pulled the box back into place from underneath, when I heard the outhouse door open. I dropped back into the pit, fearful they might have seen me. The odor was enough to gag a maggot. I had to put a hand over my mouth to keep from retchin', for fear the noise would give me away. And if that weren't insult enough to my pride, the son-bitch dropped his pants and relieved himself right on top of me! I still had my shotgun, and believe you me, I was sorely tempted to haul off and blow that bastard's bowels out the top of his skull!

"Although I couldn't see a god-damn thing, I could hear them laughin' and shoutin' as they rustled the livestock and loaded up their wagons. I made out Loretta and Dottie's voices amid the ruckus. Dottie was calling out to Jesus for help, while Loretta was crying for her daddy, bless her. Listening to that child wailin' her heart out nearly made mine break in two! I wanted to go and save them, but I was so damned scared, all I could do was stand there up to my knees in shit."

"There's nothing you could have done that would have helped the Tuckers," Hell assured him.

"Mebbe. I might be a graybeard now, but there was a day when I could look a curly wolf in the eye and make him blink. Hell, you don't get to be my age in this country and not know how to take care of yourself. It's a sad state of affairs when a man like me has to hide in a shit-hole. I tell you what, though—it was a far sight easier to crawl down there than it was to crawl up. I hadn't been free but a few minutes when I seen you sneakin' through the dooryard."

"How long do you reckon it's been since they lit out?" Hell asked.

"Judging from where the moon is now, I'd say at least two hours."

"I saw wagon tracks leading west, Sam," Pretty Woman said, confirming what Cuss had told them. "Judging from their depth, they're heavily loaded, and they're running a string of at least ten horses, besides the ones hitched to the wagons."

"Good—then there's a chance we might be able to catch him before daylight breaks. Thank you for your help, Mr. Johnson," Hell said, touching the brim of his hat. "C'mon, Pretty—time to ride!"

"Now hold on there, you two!" Cuss snarled, hurling the boot he'd been cleaning to the floor. "What about me?"

"You should be safe. Sangre and his men won't come back."

"Fuck this Sangre and the horse he rode in on! You ain't leavin' me behind like some useless piece of ol' junk! I'm goin' with you!"

Hell frowned and shook his head. "It's too dangerous, Mr. Johnson."

Cuss gave a humorless laugh. "Dangerous? What part of my life up to now has been *safe*, son? I figger I'll be endin' up in the bone orchard a lot sooner than later, no matter what. But how is that any different from what becomes of any man born of woman? It's what you do between comin' into this life and goin' out that marks you as a man. The Tuckers took me in when I was lower than a snake's dick. They're the closet thing I've ever come to havin' a family. And a man don't stand by and do squat when his family's in trouble. I figger Jimbo for a goner, but I got to trust in the Lord that it's not too late for Dottie, Loretta and the other two kids. This is my chance to do right by them."

"I can appreciate how you feel, Cuss. But I said no, and I meant it!" Hell said sternly. "Sangre on his own is deadly enough, not to mention the gang of hardened killers he's got doing his dirty work. I don't need to have a crippled up civilian in the way when things get hairy, even if he *does* have his heart in the right place. Now, if you don't mind, Mr. Johnson, Pretty and I have some riding to do if we're going to catch up with them before it's too late." With that Hell and his companion turned back in the direction of their horses.

Cuss jumped out of his chair and limped to the door of the shack, grasping the frame with both hands in order to steady himself. "I know where they're goin'!" he shouted after the retreating figures. "I overheard a couple of them jawin' while I was hiding in the biffy!"

Hell turned and glowered at the ranch hand. "Where are they headed?"

"No, *sir!*" Cuss said with a vigorous shake of his head. "I ain't gonna tell you nothin' unless you agree to take me with you!"

"I could *make* you tell me, old man," the Ranger said darkly.

"I don't doubt that. But somethin' tells me you ain't that kind of a man, partner."

"There are only two horses."

"I figger I can ride double with one of y'all."

Hell turned to look at Pretty Woman. "Your medicine got anything to say about this?"

Pretty reached into one of the pouches tied to her belt and withdrew a handful of small, polished bones and tossed them onto the ground. She squatted on her haunches and squinted at the pattern they made in the dirt at her feet. She quickly snatched the bones back up, returning them to their pouch.

"Bring him," she said, with a weary sigh. "But if you think I am going to allow that stinking old coot to ride double with me, you got another think coming."

Chapter Six

"WHEN ARE YOU GONNA TELL ME where Sangre's gang is headed?" Hell asked over his shoulder.

"When we're far enough away that I know you can't just ditch me and ride on ahead," Cuss replied. "What about you? What's this cocksucker to you?"

"Let's just say he and I have some unfinished business and leave it at that."

"You been huntin' this Sangre varmint long?"

"Longer than I'd care to remember. This is the closest I've gotten to him since I started. This is big country, and it's real easy to lose yourself in it, even for someone like Sangre. Especially if you don't want to be found."

"This 'unfinished business'—does it have somethin' to do with you bein' dead?"

"Beg pardon?" Hell said, turning around in his saddle to scowl at his passenger.

"I might not be book-learned, but I ain't dumb. You got the same pale cast to your skin as that cocksucker in the fancy vest. And then there's the fact your eyes tend to shine like a coyote's around a campfire, not to mention that I've been ridin' nuts to butt with you for the better part of an hour and I've yet to feel a heartbeat in your chest. Your skin is as cold as a rattler in January, by the way."

"You ain't scared none?" Hell asked, surprised by the old-timer's nonchalance.

"Son, I'm so scairt I could shit peach pits! But I ain't scairt of you. I like to think I can get a bead on a feller pretty good. Somethin' tells me that no matter what, at your deep-down core you're someone who can be counted on to do what's right. That's mighty hard to find in folks that are still alive, much less dead. Uh—you don't drink human blood, do you? Just askin', mind ya."

"Nope. Mostly I feed on rabbits and the like. It works out fairly well—I drain 'em, and Pretty eats 'em. Now, are you going to tell me where they are or not?"

"They're headed for Diablo Wells."

"Doesn't ring a bell."

"No reason why it should. It ain't a real settlement. Not anymore, anyways. It's located just east of the Salt Flats on the Diablo Plateau. It started out as a Spanish village. It even has a church—or what used to be one. Then there was a smallpox outbreak about thirty years back. Those that didn't die packed up and left everything behind. The whole place ain't nothin' but ruins, and it's got a reputation for bein' haunted. The wells are still there, though. The only visitors it gets anymore are occasional cowpokes lookin' to water their herds and desperadoes aimin' to avoid the law."

"Sounds like the ideal place for Sangre and his gang to hole up."

They rode on in relative silence, following the wagon tracks through the hard, dry soil of the Trans-Pecos Basin, until Hell's attention was attracted by something glittering on the ground. He reined his mount to a halt, signaling for Pretty Woman to follow suit.

"Huh—? What?" Cuss snorted, startled from a light doze. "What's wrong?"

"It's getting closer to dawn. They're lightening their load." Hell said, swinging down from his saddle in order to pick up a discarded copper pan. He walked a few more steps, kicking aside the collection of cookware littering the ground. "Seems they tossed whatever was handy out the back of the wagons."

"What's that?" Cuss asked, pointing at what looked to be a couple sacks of grain lying beneath a stunted yucca alongside the trail.

Pretty Woman trotted her pony forward to investigate. As Hell moved to join her, she gave her partner a short, sad shake of her head. Although the body was sprawled belly-down on the desert floor, they could still see its face. Something had turned the dead man's head completely around on his neck just as easy as winding a watch stem.

"What in blue blazes is going on?" Cuss had dismounted as well and was leading the horse over to where they stood. "What's so special about a few bags of oats tossed off the back of a—" His voice trailed off as he stared at the corpse. Cuss wiped his mouth with a clenched fist. "That's Jimbo," he said, his voice tight as a drumhead.

"I'm sorry, Cuss." Hell squeezed the old man's shoulder.

Cuss took a deep breath and turned his gaze skyward, as if searching it for respite from pain. "Why would someone do that to his body? Ain't it enough they kilt him?"

"It prevents Sangre's victims from coming back as dead'uns," Hell explained. "It keeps down the competition."

"We've got to bury him," Cuss said.

"That'll take too long."

"I don't care!" the old man snapped in reply. "I ain't gonna let the buzzards and coyotes scatter his bones from here to San Antonio! I owe the man that much."

"I find your loyalty admirable," Hell said. "But he's beyond caring now, Cuss."

"Yes, but I ain't."

Hell sighed and dropped his shoulders in acquiescence. "There's no time to dig a grave. You'll have to be satisfied with piling rocks on top of him."

"Thank you, Mister Hell."

"Call me Sam."

Pretty Woman folded her arms and favored her partner with a half-smile. "For someone without a heartbeat, you sure are a soft touch."

"Bite your tongue. Come on, let's lend him a hand. The sooner we get finished, the sooner we can leave."

After twenty minutes, the three had succeeded in building a cairn over the body of the late Jimbo Tucker. As Cuss placed the last rock atop the pile, he dusted his hands on his thighs and turned to face the others.

"I reckon this is as good a time as any to confess that I ain't been honest with y'all."

"How so?" Hell asked, raising an eyebrow.

"What I said about Jimbo helpin' me when I was down and out was true enough. But I lied to you about how I got my leg busted up. I weren't a hand on the Lazy J. I was a gunrunner. I sold mostly to the Apache, or anyone else who could meet my price. Then, five years ago, I made the mistake of takin' on a real asshole for a partner. He decided he could make out a hell of lot better without havin' to split the profits with me. So the bastard snuck up on me while I was sleepin' one night and broke my leg with an axe handle, then left me out in the desert to die. It was Jimbo Tucker who found me, more dead than alive, and brought me home.

"He and his wife nursed me back to health, even after I told 'em the truth about myself. I was a sinner—one of the worst ever born— yet they forgave me my trespasses and offered me a chance to live an honest life. I didn't have no family to speak of as a young'un, so I've pretty much made my own way since I was a boy. The world ain't shown me much kindness. But the Tuckers . . ." Cuss stopped and cleared his throat. "The Tuckers did good by me. And I figure to do good by 'em. I'm gonna do my damnedest to make sure that Dottie, Katie, young Jimmy and Loretta make it out of this alive, even if it means I die tryin'."

All that was left of Diablo Wells was a collection of single-story adobes gathered at the foot of a small hill, on top of which sat a church, whose badly cracked whitewashed stucco facade revealed the red mud bricks underneath. The wells that gave the village its name and reason for existence were still in evidence, located in the center of what had once been the town square.

At the edge of the ghost town were two corrals constructed of the same red mud bricks as the rest of the village. One contained the horses stolen from Tucker's Station. The other housed the passengers from the stage and what remained of the Tucker family.

From his vantage behind an outcropping of rock and cactus, Hell could see that the women were doing their best to console the frightened youngsters, who ranged in age from seven to fifteen years of age. While the women and children were free to move about, the men had their hands tied behind their backs and ropes looped about their necks, like a string of prize bulls ready for market.

One of Sangre's followers sat on the corral wall, a cocked rifle in his hands, watching the prisoners with the detached air of a bored wrangler. Every so often, he would cast a look over his shoulder in the direction of his fellow bandits, who were whooping it up back in the village.

The two female members of the gang, one a strawberry blonde, the other a brunette, were outfitted in new dresses taken from the trading post. Their male counterparts were eagerly downing bottles of trade whisky as they shouted and sang. The brunette was dancing with one of the men, while another played a guitar. As Hell watched, the strawberry blonde hiked her skirts up over her hips and took one of her partners in crime, a large man with a scarred face, between her legs. The others clapped their hands and whistled loudly, urging on their companion's rut with rude comments and raucous laughter.

Suddenly there was an abrupt hush as the bandits halted their revelry in mid-debauchery, their heads turning in the same direction, as if connected to a string. Hell saw Sangre standing framed in the doorway of one of the adobes. The conquistador snapped his fingers and pointed to the corrals. The scar-faced man fucking the strawberry blonde nodded and pulled up his pants, leaving the others to resume their carousing. His place atop the woman was quickly taken by one of his fellows, who picked up where he had left off.

Sangre strode purposefully toward the pen where the humans were being held, his hands clasped in the small of his back. Upon reaching the corral, the scar-faced man retrieved a four-foot-long catchpole. After properly adjusting the noose of rope at the pole's far end, he stood by and waited for his master to make his pick.

The Spaniard methodically stroked his chin as he studied the assembled prisoners before pointing to the little girl. The scar-faced man nodded and hopped over the wall as if he were setting out to rope a calf for branding.

"*No!*" Dottie Tucker screamed at the approaching outlaw. "Don't you dare touch her!"

Dottie grabbed Loretta, trying to put herself between her daughter and the monster that had killed her husband. But Loretta was so frightened she wriggled free of her mother's grip and dashed across the corral. Even though she was small and fast, she never stood a chance. The scar-faced man was on her like duck on a June bug.

"*Mamaaa!*" Loretta screamed as the catchpole's noose dropped about her neck.

Her screams for help were choked off as the scar-faced wrangler pulled on the slack end of the rope. Her legs folded under her as her fingers clawed at the rope cinched tight about her throat.

"Let her go, you son of a bitch!" Cuss bellowed as he broke cover, standing up to fire upon the scar-faced bandit, catching him between the eyes.

"Goddamn it, you old coot! I told you to hold your fire until I gave the signal!" Hell shouted in exasperation. Now that their cover was blown, he had no choice but to follow the retired gunrunner's lead. What he had intended no longer mattered. They were committed to action now, and extreme action at that.

Hell, Cuss and Pretty Woman charged the corral. Pretty Woman put a bullet into the armed guard, knocking him off the wall. Cuss fired at the conquistador, striking him in the chest, but Sangre didn't so much as blink. Sangre bared his fangs and moved forward, sneering his disdain for his attackers.

"Don't waste your ammo on him!" Hell yelled. "Let me handle Sangre."

He fired his pistol, catching the conquistador in the right shoulder. Where the previous bullet seemed to have no effect, this time Sangre shrieked like a cat and clutched his left arm. There was anger in the conquistador's scarlet eyes, but also fear. Never before had he been wounded by a conventional weapon.

Hell raised his pistol higher for a headshot but was distracted by the volley of gunfire from the direction of the village. Sangre's followers had tossed aside the liquor in favor of their guns and were rushing to their master's aid.

Pretty Woman threw open the gate to the horse pen and fired her pistol over her head. The frightened animals bolted forth, charging right for the onrushing bandits. The strawberry blonde screamed as she disappeared under the hooves of the stampeding livestock. Upon seeing the chaos before him, Sangre tossed back his head and gave voice to a cry so high-pitched it was more felt than heard.

"What in the devil is he doing?" The stage driver asked as Hell freed his hands.

"Calling for reinforcements," the Dark Ranger replied, as pale, gaunt-faced figures emerged from the shadows of the ruined buildings, their eyes gleaming in the dark. "We have to get to the church—*fast!*"

Sangre's unholy offspring were an odd mix of gamblers, Indian braves, dancehall girls, horse thieves and school marms, most of whom were still dressed in the clothes they had died in. Hell gave up counting when he reached thirty.

"Get to the church! All of you!" he shouted.

"What about you, Sam?" Cuss asked.

"Don't worry about me. As long as I'm wearing this, I'll be okay in there," he replied, tapping the bloodstone we wore about his neck. "I just need you to get these people to safety."

The newly freed prisoners did as they were told, running as fast as they could up the hill. However, Katie Tucker made the mistake of looking behind her. When she saw the legion of dead'uns at the base of the hill she screamed and lost her footing. Pretty Woman heard the girl cry out looked back to see her sprawled on the ground, paralyzed by fear as Sangre's spawn swarmed up the hill. Cursing under her breath, the medicine woman reversed her course.

"Damn it, child! If you want to live, get up!" Pretty Woman barked, grabbing the girl's upper arm.

"I—can't! I'm too scared!" Kate sobbed.

"Don't look at them! Look at *me!*" Pretty Woman shouted, jerking Katie to her feet. "Now run, and don't stop!"

Katie lurched up the hillside, alternately sobbing and gasping. Even though her heart was beating so fast it felt like she had a hummingbird stuck between her ribs, she did as the Comanche shamaness told her. She did not look back until she reached the door of the church, where her mother and younger brother were waiting for her. Only then did she turn around, just in time to see Pretty Woman disappear under a mass of pale, dead flesh.

The interior of the church was empty save for some wooden pews, an altar located in the nave and a full-sized wooden cross hanging from the wall above it. The stained glass windows had long since been destroyed by the ravages of time, leaving the floor covered with rainbow-colored shards of glass.

"Is everyone here and accounted for?" Hell asked, a concerned look on his face. "Where's Pretty Woman?"

"I fell down and she came back to get me and—and—" Katie burst into tears, burying her face in her hands. "They were all over her!"

Though the news hit Hell like a kidney punch, he tried his best not to let it show. He was surrounded by frightened, confused people way out of their depth, and they were all looking to him to get them out of the situation they were in. He had to keep up a strong facade, or the others would come unraveled like so much bad knitting.

"We've got to barricade ourselves the best we can. I need you, Clem, and you, Elmer," he pointed to the stage driver and his assistant, "to move these pews in front of the doors. And I want you two to try and do the same with the windows," he said, pointing to Mr. Crocker and the salesman.

"Why bother? We're doomed, no matter what!" The salesman spat, kicking at the shards of colored glass that littered the floor. "This being a holy place might keep the hell-beasts at bay, but it won't slow down the others."

"That's no way to be talkin' in front of the women and kids!" Cuss snapped. "Now you do as Sam says, or I'll toss you outside myself! You savvy me, slick?"

61

The salesman opened his mouth to argue, but there was something in the old-timer's eyes that made him decide against it. Grumbling under his breath, he set about his task.

Cuss took Hell's elbow and pulled him away from the others. "Remember I told you I was a gunrunner? That's the reason I know about Diablo Wells in the first place. Last time I was here was just before my lowdown snake of a partner tried to turn my leg into firewood. I had a feelin' he was up to something, so I hid a cache of guns here, just in case he tried to run off with all the goods."

"Lot of good that does us stuck here," Hell sighed.

"Son, when I said I hid them here, that's exactly what I meant." Cuss grinned, pointing at the altar. "The inside's hollow. Help me move the lid. It's damned heavy, but it comes off."

Mrs. Crocker, who had been doing her best to comfort the weeping Katie, frowned her disapproval as the two men laid hands on the altar. "Here now! What are you two doing? That's the Lord's table!"

"And the Lord helps those who help themselves, my good lady," Cuss said, touchin' the battered brim of his hat before returning to his task.

"I'll get it," Hell said, lifting the heavy oaken altar top as if it were made from balsa wood.

Cuss peered into the interior of the altar and let loose with a whoop. Inside were a box of rifles and two cases of ammunition. "*Hallelujah!* We might not exactly be shittin' in high cotton, my friend," the old gunrunner said with a grin. "But at least they can't see us from the road!"

As Cuss distributed the guns among the men, Hell climbed onto an upended pew to look out one of the windows, and what he saw was enough to make his heart skip a beat, if it weren't already as still as a stone.

The church was ringed by Sangre's spawn, who kept about six feet of distance, as if held back by an invisible barrier. They muttered and moaned among themselves, staring at the church with an awful hunger in their crimson eyes. Sam had first thought Sangre's men had stolen the horses and the rest of the livestock from the trading post for their own uses, but now he realized it was to feed their master's progeny.

"¡Salga de mi manera, los tontos!"

The pallid hungry faces parted, allowing Sangre to stride forward. His left arm was in a makeshift sling fashioned from a bandana. The conquistador was accompanied by two of his human servants, who held between them the limp figure of Pretty Woman. Her head had dropped forward, so her hair obscured her face. The toes of her moccasins dragged the ground behind her.

"*Ranger!*" Sangre shouted. "Ranger, do you hear me?"

"Yeah, I hear you!" Hell yelled back.

"As you can see, I have *su puta india*. It was all I could do to keep my followers from eating or raping her—if not both. As for myself—I do not think I will make her one of my brides. She is too headstrong, and willful women never make good wives." Sangre grabbed Pretty Woman's hair, pulling her head back so Hell could see her bruised and swollen face. "However, I think her skin would make an excellent leather vest—do you not agree?"

"Damn you! What do you want?"

"The same thing you want from me, Ranger—to look you eye-to-eye as I kill you! But I am willing to make you an offer, *mi amigo*. I will spare *la india* if you are willing to come forward, and meet me, *mano a mano*."

"Why should I believe you?"

"What choice do you have? You do as I say, or the squaw dies now." Sangre motioned to one of the bandits, who pulled a machete from his belt and positioned the blade against Pretty Woman's exposed jugular. "Either way, it is your decision."

"Very well! I'm coming out!" Hell replied, jumping down from his perch.

Cuss and the other men were gathered by the front door. "What are you doin', Sam?" the old man asked. "It's a trap!"

"I know. But I have no choice. You told me you had to do right by the Tuckers—well, it's the same for me and Pretty Woman. I've got to try and get her back. Just shut the door as fast as you can and make sure that barricade stays in place. If it's a trap, don't hesitate to open fire. Don't worry about shooting the dead'uns, just focus on the living bastards working for Sangre, otherwise you're just wasting ammo. I'm counting on you to hold the fort until dawn. That shouldn't be more than a couple of hours from now. If you can make it to sunrise, then everything else will seem like a cakewalk."

"I got you, Sam. Good luck out there, partner."

"Same here."

The doors to the old church opened just wide enough to allow Hell to step out. The sound of the barricade being quickly put back in place behind him was as final as Judgment Day.

Chapter Seven

AS HELL STRODE to where Sangre stood waiting for him, the dead'uns drew back, quivering like whipped dogs. One of the human bandits stepped forward and aimed his pistol at Hell's head. He froze, shooting an angry look in the direction of the Spaniard.

"I thought you said this was to be *mano a mano.*"

"And so it shall be, *mi amigo,*" Sangre said with a crooked smile. "But first, please be so kind as to hand over your gun belt. I do not know what sorcery you have used to charm the bullets in your gun, and I do not intend to suffer any further wounding at your hand in such a manner."

Hell glowered as he unfastened his holsters and gun belt and handed them over to the bandit pointing the gun at his head.

"You have proven yourself a worthy adversary, Ranger," Sangre admitted. "Ah! I see you are surprised that I know of you. How could I not, when each time you destroy one of my disciples, I, too, feel the wound, one step removed? As one of the undead, you know that all I create are bound to me by blood. And that includes you. I made a gross mistake when I did not hunt you down and destroy you the night you escaped Golgotha. Like the living, the undead are made in their maker's image. Yet not all of my spawn are created equal. Most are weak-minded, sheep-like creatures, good for nothing more than cannon fodder. Feeding may spread the seed of our kind, but such promiscuity dilutes the breed. That's why I, alone, feed on humans, while the others must make do with horses and livestock.

"Humans of strong character and powerful will are rarely good choices for resurrection, because they are the ones who weary of servitude and eventually challenge their maker for control. Those prone to virtue also make very poor spawn. Take that dreary little man from the trading post, for example. I drained him as needed, but I denied him rebirth in my image. As for you, *mi amigo*, I sensed you were too strong-willed, too 'good' to be gifted with eternal life. But I was still giddy with freedom after spending centuries folded like a suit of old clothes, and allowed you to escape.

"I came to this accursed new world with Cortes, our hearts burning for gold and glory. But where he was proclaimed a god, I was declared a devil. Not that I did not give them good cause to think so. It was the Indian slaves who first gave me the name 'Sangre,' you know. I heard stories of a tribe of wizard-priests dedicated to Xipe Totec, god of the Aztec goldsmiths, said to be guardians of a great treasure. I took my men and went in search of their temple. It took me several months, and I lost many of my men to fever and jaguars, but in the end I found them. The wizard-priests claimed to be the result of the mating of human women and gods. Perhaps that is true, for they all possessed six fingers and toes. But if they had divine blood in their veins, it did not save them.

"I roasted each and every one of them alive, turning them on spits above a pit of coals like suckling pigs, but still they refused to tell me where they had hidden their gold. Their high priest cursed me, saying that he would turn the invaders' sword upon them, then spat in my eye just before he died. When I returned to Cortes empty-handed and told him what I had done, he had me clapped in irons. Not long after that, I was placed in the stockade, where I fell ill from a fever and died. But I did not stay dead.

"Three days after I was buried, I clawed my way free of my grave. It did not take long before Cortes and his followers realized there was a demin in their midst. My plan was to remake the entire Aztec Empire in my image and name myself their demon-king. Once I secured my hold on the New World, I would do the same to the Old. All this was within my reach, if not for Cortes's concubine, that wretched whore Malinche.

"She was the one who coerced the old Aztec wizard into helping her lover defeat me. At first the sorcerer saw no reason to do anything to benefit the invaders. But when she claimed that Huitzilopochtli, the sun god, would punish the Aztec for turning their face from his shining countenance in favor of eternal darkness, he relented and cast the spell that created the bloodstone.

"Malinche knew that since I had lusted after her in life, I would eventually come for her in death. She pretended to lay sleeping as I slipped into her hut. As I leaned forward to take her blood, she sat up and placed the charmed amulet about my neck. I was instantly rendered powerless and fell onto the floor motionless. Although I was still in possession of all my senses and knew everything that transpired about me, I was unable to move or speak.

"Cortes and the others did not know how to destroy me. After all, how do you kill something that is already dead? So they elected to lock me away and hide me in a place where I would never be found. I was placed in an iron box, the protection of which was assigned to Cortes's most trusted servant, Garcia. He was given a wagon, provisions, horses, a couple of Indian slaves, as well as a saddlebag full of gold, and was told to go as far away as humanly possible and never return.

"And so I spent three hundred years trapped in eternal darkness, immobile yet still aware of my surroundings. I felt my skin wither and the flesh rot from my bones while being tormented by a dreadful thirst that burned in my belly, just like the coals I used to roast that accursed six-fingered priest! I would have probably stayed buried until the sun dwindled to a cinder, if not for those fools searching for water.

"I am far older and wiser now. I shall have my empire, but I shall take my time building it. The mistake I made before was thinking in terms of human spans. Because of that, I exposed myself to the cattle on which I preyed, and gave sworn enemies a chance to unify against a greater threat. I know better, now. What are years, even decades, to one who measures his existence in centuries?"

Hell spat into the dirt at his feet in disgust. "So, are we gonna get on with this, or are you gonna keep jawing?"

"I had hoped that you, of all my spawn, might be able to appreciate what I had to say," Sangre grimaced. "But I see you are as thick-witted as the rest of the natives of this wretched continent! But before we continue, you must rid yourself of that horrid bauble you wear about your neck."

Hell looked over at Pretty Woman. The left side of her face was so swollen it looked as if someone had managed to shove a small rubber ball under her eyelid. She turned her head slightly, so that she could see him with her good eye, and mouthed the word 'no'. Hell's fingers closed about the medallion, pulling it free from around his neck with a single yank, and let it drop to the ground.

As the bloodstone fell from his grasp, he was overcome by a rage so intense and all encompassing it tinged everything red, as if someone had dipped everyone and everything around him in blood. It was as if he had been standing on the beach and a great wave had suddenly come up from nowhere and crashed down on him, dragging him out to sea. He could not see, hear or breathe, and he could not regain his footing as he fought against the tide. But instead of water, he was surrounded by a fearsome darkness, and the harder he struggled, the more he drowned.

His belly burned as if packed with hot sand, and his tongue felt as if it was made of jerked beef. The agony was so intense he cried out, burying his face in his hands. He knew he would do whatever it might take to quench the thirst raging within him, even if it meant crawling on his belly through barbed wire and broken glass. Suddenly a voice broke through the screeching white noise that filled his head. When it spoke the words were like a cool hand on a feverish brow.

You need not suffer so. All that is needed to end the pain is a little blood. Drink from the woman. Her blood is yours. Take it, my son.

Hell lifted his face from his hands and stared at the Indian woman before him. A part of him found her familiar, but he could not push aside the fire in his gut long enough to think of where he knew her from.

Her blood will be sweeter than any wine. It will slake your thirst and make you strong. Drink deep, my son, and bind yourself to my service for all eternity.

Hell slowly approached the trembling woman. Although she struggled mightily to escape, she was unable to free herself from the two strong men pinning her arms behind her back. Her one good eye was wide with terror, and the fear coursing through her body made her carotid artery pulse even faster. If he concentrated, he could hear her blood rushing through her veins, pumping through her racing heart. It was as if it were calling out to him, begging him to set it free.

He leaned forward, brushing his cheek against the side of her head. She involuntarily gasped and held her breath. Her perfume was a heady mixture of fear and sweat. Something buried deep inside Sam Hell stirred, twisting about like a snake trapped in a jar.

"*Sam,*" the woman whispered, a solitary tear trickling from her good eye.

Hell grabbed her by the hair, jerking back her head so that she could see his face as he grinned, exposing his teeth. He opened his mouth wide, arching his neck like a cobra preparing to spit its venom—and sank his fangs deep into the throat of the man holding Pretty Woman's right arm.

The bandit screamed and let go of his captive in a desperate attempt to pull himself free. With a savage sidewise shaking of his head, Hell tore open the bandit's jugular vein. The blood that spurted into his mouth tasted sweet, quenching the fire in his guts. Part of him wanted to keep drinking until his skin was as full and tight as a tick's, but he forced himself to stop for fear of losing himself in a feeding frenzy. The mortally wounded bandit fell to the ground, one hand clamped over the pumping gash in his throat, blood squirting between his fingers like water from a hose.

The smell of spilled blood was making the assembled dead'uns increasingly agitated. An undead dancehall girl leapt onto the wounded bandit before he had a chance to scream, and within seconds he was buried under a writhing carpet of pale, dead flesh. The dead'uns snarled and snapped at one another like a pack of jackals as they fought to feed.

"*Madre de Dios!*" exclaimed the bandit holding Pretty Woman's left arm, recoiling from the sight of his comrade being ripped to shreds.

The second her remaining captor loosened his grip, Pretty Woman turned on him, slamming the heel of her palm into his nasal bridge while bringing her knee into his groin. He went down hard, cupping his hands over his shattered nose. He had time to scream only once before he, too, was swarmed.

"Run for it, Pretty!" Hell shouted before he disappeared under a sea of grasping hands and flailing limbs. "*Run!*"

The shamaness sprinted toward the church with two of Sangre's human followers on her heels. Suddenly there was a hail of gunfire from the church, dropping one of the bandits dead in his tracks, and causing the second to dive for cover. The door to the church opened, and Pretty Woman darted inside. Cuss and Clem continued to lay down fire from the windows while the rest of the men hurriedly replaced the barricade.

Once she was safely inside and the doorway was blocked once again, Cuss handed his rifle over to Elmer and dropped down from his sniper's perch. "Good to have you back, Missy."

"It's good to be back, Cuss. But this is far from over. Sam's still out there, and in greater danger than any of us could possibly imagine. I've got to help him." She went over to where the Tucker children were busily loading the spare rifles with ammunition. "Girl!" she said, pointing at Katie. "You must answer the question I am about to ask truthfully: Have you ever been with a man?"

The young girl's cheeks turned bright pink and she her eyes.

"What kind of question is that for a squaw to ask a god-fearin' white girl?" Mrs. Tucker said indignantly.

"Stay out of this!" Pretty Woman snapped. "It is for the girl to answer!"

"It's okay, mama," Katie said. "I owe her my life. I can answer her question. No: I've never been with a man. Not the way you mean, anyway."

"Good," Pretty Woman replied, taking out her knife and slashing it across the young girl's palm. "Then we stand a chance. But we'll still need a distraction."

"¡Bastante!" Sangre shouted, angrily kicking the seething mass of undead flesh before him. "Stop it, you mindless fools! Stop it before I destroy you all!" The dead'uns quickly retreated, trembling before their creator's rage like cowed dogs fearful of their master's lash. "Get him on his feet!" Sangre snarled, pointing to Hell's prone body.

Two dead'uns obediently grabbed the former Ranger and jerked him upright.

"We undead are a hardy breed," Sangre said, retrieving the knife tucked into his boot. "We break a leg and it knits within hours. Pluck out our eyes, and they grow back in a fortnight. While we cannot regenerate severed limbs, or survive a fire, for all practical purposes we are immortal. That can be both a blessing and a curse. As you will soon discover.

"I shall have you drawn and quartered, so that you can never again raise a hand against me or run away from me. Then I shall have your eyes gouged out, your ears cut off and your nose sliced off." Sangre mimed the actions with short, sharp jabs of his knife. "I will keep you in your own little box, like I was kept. And whenever your eyes, ears and nose start to grow back, I will have them removed yet again. And again. And again!" Sangre pressed the flat of the blade against Hell's cheek, angling the tip so that it was directly under his right eye. "Perhaps then you will learn your lesson, eh?"

"Lord Sangre!" one of the bandits blurted. "Something's happening at the mission!"

The conquistador turned to see the double doors of the church swing wide open and Cuss Johnson come barreling out, bellowing at the top of his lungs, a huge wooden cross clutched in his hands like a battle standard. Sangre's spawn, made bold by their feeding frenzy, surged forward, shrieking in delight at the prospect of another meal, only to have the first of their number that came within striking distance of the cross burst into flame like dry kindling.

"Come on, you sorry sons of bitches!" Cuss yelled as he swung the cross like a giant baseball bat. "Come and get it!"

The dead'uns drew back, their hunger overridden by their sense of self-preservation. Since the enemy was refusing to attack, the former gunrunner waded in among them, swatting them like so many flies. "Hold on, Sam!" he shouted as he set an Apache dead'un ablaze with a backhand swing. "I'm comin'!"

Sangre cursed and motioned for his remaining human servants, who were gawking at the sight before them with open mouths, to close ranks around him. "What are you fools waiting for?" he shouted. "Shoot him!"

The bandits opened fire and Cuss went down in a hail of bullets, the cross falling from his hands before he hit the ground. Hell used the distraction to break free and run to where his friend lay dying on the hard earth. Without a moment's hesitation, the Dark Ranger snatched up the fallen cross.

Though he was wearing leather gloves, he could feel his hands grow hot the moment he touched the icon. Screaming in anger, grief and pain, he charged toward Sangre, who stood behind his wall of human killers. He could feel bullets enter his chest and belly, but they meant nothing to him and hurt even less. Smoke curled from his palms as he brought the cross down onto a bandit's skull, and he put the searing pain in his hands out of his mind. As he flailed away, all he could see in his mind's eye was his father, desperately chopping at the rattlesnake that had bitten him before it had a chance to slither away and kill someone else.

The bandits protecting Sangre fell away, their heads crushed and necks fractured, until there was nothing separating Sam Hell from Sangre. He swung the cross high above his head, but as he was about to bring it down with all his might, his leather gloves dissolved in a burst of flame, setting his hands afire. Though Hell tried to maintain his hold on the cross, the agony was too great. He dropped the wooden icon to the ground, where it continued to burn. Gasping in pain, Hell dropped to his knees, holding his charred hands before him in a grotesque parody of prayer. The skin was blackened, like that of roasted meat, with deep fissures that exposed the bones underneath.

Sangre stepped forward, amused by the turn of events. "You continue to amaze me, Ranger. You are damned, yet you seek to walk in the light. You battle against your own kind in the name of a deity who has turned his countenance from you. It is utter folly to deny what you are, to fight against the dictates of your nature—and yet you continue to do so, even when you know it is hopeless. You are either a deluded fool or the bravest man to have graced this planet. Either way, you are far too dangerous for me to allow you to continue to exist, even as a pet torso."

Sangre retrieved Hell's gun belt and removed the revolver from its holster, holding it so that the barrel pointed to the sky like a steel finger. "If your bullets have enough magic in them to wound the immortal, then they must also be able to kill them."

The conquistador aimed the barrel directly at Hell's forehead. Hell wanted to pray, but he knew that the words would burn in his mouth, so he closed his eyes instead.

Suddenly Sangre paused, a confused look on his face. He tilted his head to one side, then another, sniffing the air like a hound trying to identify a scent. "Do you smell that?"

"Smell what, my lord?" replied a dead'un with a United States Marshal's star pinned to his vest.

"Brine."

A flash of lightning abruptly tore across the night sky, immediately followed by a crash of thunder. Thinking he'd been shot, Hell opened his eyes and looked around, surprised that his brains were still in his head. A strong wind had come from nowhere, kicking up dust devils that danced among the assembled dead'uns, tugging on their clothes and hair like unruly children.

Fat raindrops struck the dusty ground hard enough to be heard. Instinctively, Sangre lifted his head to stare up at the clouds overhead. As a raindrop struck his cheek, the skin began to bubble and sizzle. The Spaniard screamed and clutched his face. His shriek was quickly picked up and echoed by his spawn, who also began to claw at their flesh like things possessed.

A raindrop struck the back of Hell's neck, burning the exposed skin like a drop of hydrochloric acid. As he leapt to his feet, yowling in pain, the Ranger saw Pretty Woman running out of the church, a bundle under one arm. Upon reaching him, she threw a man's jacket over his head.

"Mr. Crocker was nice enough to loan you this. Don't take it off, if you want to keep your skull in one piece!" she warned.

"The bloodstone—I can't go back inside the church without it," Hell gasped.

"I already have it." The medicine woman held up the amulet and quickly looped it around his neck. "I snatched it without them noticing when I escaped."

"*Bruja!* You are the one responsible for this!" Sangre shrieked, great beads of liquid fat rolling from his face like tallow from a candle. He pointed an accusing finger at Pretty Woman, the flesh dripping from it as if he had just dipped his hand in honey. "This is no natural storm! ¡Mátelos todo!" Sangre screamed as his face sloughed away, revealing the skull underneath.

If Sangre's army of the night heard him, they gave no sign of it as they darted about frantically, their flesh running from their bones. Those who had lost their eyes to the mysterious downpour stumbled into the fellows, causing them to trip and fall into pools of rainwater mixed with viscera, where they continued to dissolve even faster than before. Elmer and Mr. Crocker stood in the open doorway, watching the destruction of Sangre and his unholy legion with a mixture of disgust and fascination.

"My God," Mr. Crocker said. "It's like when my wife pours salt on the slugs in our garden."

Pretty Woman hurried her charge past the two men guarding the door and into the safety of the waiting church. As Hell tossed aside the jacket that had protected him from the murderous downpour, the others closed in about him.

"Cuss told us what Sangre did to you," Jimmy Tucker said, fixing Hell with a curious eye. "He said that you were like those things outside, but different. Is that true?"

"Yes, son. It's true," Hell said with a slight smile that showed his fangs.

"Well, I don't care if you are one of them things, you saved my life, mister—and I want to shake your hand!" The salesman said, thrusting his hand forward. He froze when he saw the blackened ruins jutting out of the end of Hell's shirt cuffs.

"Dear Lord!" Mrs. Crocker gasped.

"Don't worry, ma'am, "Hell said with a weak smile. "I'll be good as new in just a few hours."

Loretta Tucker jumped up and pointed in the direction of the door. "Mama! Look! It's Cuss!"

Hell turned and saw the old gunrunner standing in the door of the church, rainwater and blood pouring down the front of his clothes. Elmer and Clem ran to help their friend into the building, where he was placed in one of the pews, a folded petticoat under his head. Dottie Tucker sat down beside him, holding his hand while her children stood by and watched.

Hell leaned over and spoke the dying man's name. Cuss' eyelids flickered open and he gave the Ranger a weak smile. "Hey there, Sam. Glad to see you got back safe."

"Good Lord, Cuss—why did you risk such a damn fool stunt just to save me?"

"Seemed like the thing to do at the time," the old man rasped, attempting a shrug. "But before I go—I just want you to know, Sam, that you're a better man dead than most folks livin.'"

"Back at you, partner," Hell whispered as he closed his friend's eyes.

Chapter Eight

HELL AWOKE TO FIND HIMSELF lying flat on his back, staring up at the underside of a church pew. He crawled out from his makeshift shelter and stretched his stiff muscles with an audible crack. The interior of the church was deserted save for Pretty Woman, who was seated crossed-legged atop the altar.

"Where is everybody?"

"They returned to Tucker's Station after they buried Cuss," Pretty Woman explained. "They took the bandits' wagons and horses. I told Mrs. Tucker where we buried her husband along the trail, so she could bring him home, too."

"Good. I'm glad they made it out of this okay. How are you feeling, by the way?"

"Like I was kicked in the head by a buffalo." She unfolded her legs and hopped onto the ground. "So—do you want to see what's left of him?"

"Might as well get it over with," he sighed.

Hell gave out with a low whistle as he surveyed the hillside outside the church. The ground was littered with dozens of skeletons, their bleached bones gleaming silver in the West Texas moonlight.

"Which one is his?"

"That one," she said, pointing to a skeleton dressed in a fancy embroidered vest with one arm still fixed in a sling. It still held Hell's pistol clutched in its bony hand.

"I'll take that back, if you don't mind," Hell said, retrieving his weapon and gun belt. He stared at Sangre's peeled skull for a moment before bringing his boot heel down, reducing it to powder. "Mind telling me how you managed to pull off that little rain dance of yours?" he asked, as he refastened his gun belt.

"I remembered Cuss saying something about the Salt Flats being near here," Pretty Woman replied. "All I needed was the blood of a virgin and the right words to appease the spirits. Once that was done, it was relatively easy to create a strong enough wind to mix a cloud of salt dust with a rain cloud. Luckily Mrs. Tucker's oldest girl isn't a liar."

"You never cease to amaze me, Pretty, even after all this time!" Hell chuckled, shaking his head in admiration.

"Now that you've finally hunted down and killed Sangre, what are you going to do now, Sam?"

"Keep doing what I've been doing, I guess," he shrugged. "From what Sangre said, these weren't the only spawn he created. I bet he's done what he did in Golgotha a hundred times over: create an angry mob of dead'uns, then force them to fight it out among themselves until they were winnowed down to the meanest of the lot, then sent them out into the world to spread his contagion. Sangre may be gone, but the evil he created is still out there. I can feel it." Hell turned to look at Pretty Woman. "But what about you? You said your destiny was tied to Sangre's and my own. Now that he's gone, you're free to go back to your people."

"Yes, that's true," the medicine woman admitted.

"Well, are you? Going to go back, that is?"

"My people have their own path to walk, just as I have mine. For the time being, my path is the same as yours."

"I'm glad to hear that," Hell said with a smile. "Because I've gotten used to having you around." He reached up and touched the bolo tie cinched about his neck. "After all, you're one of my two lucky charms."

"You don't really need that thing, you know," she said. "When you removed it you were able to reclaim your mind and free yourself from the bloodlust. The reason the bloodstone rendered Sangre powerless was because he was evil even before he became a dead'un. When the evil within him was made dormant, he was unable to so much as move. The fact you are talking to me now proves that what evil exists inside you is far outweighed by the good."

"I know that," Hell nodded. "I guess I always have. Still, I think I'll keep it just the same. Lord knows I can use all the help I can get, even if it is from some Aztec god whose name I can't pronounce."

"Are you afraid of being tempted?"

"Of course I'm afraid! After all, I'm only human," he said with a wink of his blood-red eye. "Besides, if I get rid of it, what am I going to use to cinch my tie? Now, if you don't mind, I've got a twitch in my foot that tells me there's a poltergeist due north of here."

"Not another one!" Pretty Woman groaned. "The last time we broke one of those things, I got a chamber pot hurled at me from across the room!"

"It's too late to back out now," Hell said with a crooked grin, exposing his fangs "The Dark Ranger rides again!"

About the Author

NANCY A. COLLINS has authored more than twenty novels and novellas and numerous short stories. She has also worked on several comic books, including a two-year run on the Swamp Thing series. She is a recipient of the Bram Stoker Award and the British Fantasy Award, and has been nominated for the Eisner, John W. Campbell Memorial, and International Horror Guild Awards. Best known for her groundbreaking vampire series Sonja Blue, which heralded the rise of the popular urban fantasy genre, Collins is the author of the bestselling *Sunglasses After Dark*, the Southern Gothic collection *Knuckles and Tales*, the Vamps series for young adults, and the critically acclaimed Golgotham urban fantasy series. She currently resides in Norfolk, Virginia.

NANCY A. COLLINS

FROM OPEN ROAD MEDIA

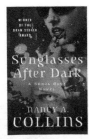

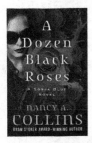

OPEN ROAD

INTEGRATED MEDIA

INTEGRATED MEDIA

Find a full list of our authors and
titles at www.openroadmedia.com

FOLLOW US
@OpenRoadMedia

Printed in the USA
CPSIA information can be obtained
at www.ICGtesting.com
LVHW041449171123
764237LV00046B/637